## Praise for the historical fiction of Fred Bean

### Eden

"Well-paced, readable, vivid."
—Larry McMurtry, *New York Times* bestselling author
of *Lonesome Dove*

### Lorena

"This fast-paced historical novel set during the last
bloody months of the Civil War is a well-crafted
blend of action and romance. Bean's research is solid,
and he is at his best re-creating the horrors of war.
The novel never loses balance or focus."
—*Publishers Weekly*

"[Fred Bean] has taken a historical incident and
caused you to relive it. . . . It's a great story."
—*The Sentinel* (Ft. Worth, TX)

### Poncho and Black Jack

"Fred Bean takes a little-known piece of American
history and he makes it live and breathe. Black Jack
Pershing, young George Patton, and Pancho Villa
come alive on the pages. Well done."
—John Byrne Cook, author of *The Snowblind Moon*

# HELL ON
# THE BORDER

J. M. Thompson
and
Fred Bean

A SIGNET BOOK

SIGNET
Published by New American Library, a division of
Penguin Putnam Inc., 375 Hudson Street,
New York, New York 10014, U.S.A.
Penguin Books Ltd, 80 Strand,
London WC2R 0RL, England
Penguin Books Australia Ltd, Ringwood,
Victoria, Australia
Penguin Books Canada Ltd, 10 Alcorn Avenue,
Toronto, Ontario, Canada M4V 3B2
Penguin Books (N.Z.) Ltd, 182–190 Wairau Road,
Auckland 10, New Zealand

Penguin Books Ltd, Registered Offices:
Harmondsworth, Middlesex, England

First published by Signet, an imprint of New American Library,
a division of Penguin Putnam Inc.

First Printing, January 2002
10  9  8  7  6  5  4  3  2  1

 REGISTERED TRADEMARK—MARCA REGISTRADA

Printed in the United States of America

PUBLISHER'S NOTE
This is a work of fiction. Names, characters, places, and incidents either
are the product of the author's imagination or are used fictitiously,
and any resemblance to actual persons, living or dead, business
establishments, events, or locales is entirely coincidental.

Just after this manuscript was finished, my writing partner and best friend, Frederic Bean, was called to the last round-up. A true friend, a gifted writer and teacher of writing, he will be sorely missed by all of his fans and all of his many friends in and out of the writing profession. We'll miss you, pal, and we'll ride again together, someday . . .
JMT

# Prologue

It was a blistering day in Fort Smith, Arkansas.
The hangman's platform, made of wood and
painted stark white, was surrounded by a fence
enclosing almost an acre of dry, parched grass.
The white-hot sun above seemed to suck the very
life out of the air and the several hundred people
gathered in the enclosure to watch the hanging.
Enterprising vendors, dressed in garish suits and
wearing derby hats, hawked everything from tiny
dolls with nooses around their necks to lukewarm
lemonade and beer. Hard liquor was forbidden at
hangings, but the local saloons did a large business in small bottles that would fit in coat pockets
to be sipped to ward off the terrible heat of Arkansas in the summer.

Six horsehair ropes hung from an overhead
beam, dangling like tree snakes waiting to claim
unwary prey. A tall, lean man dressed all in black
stood next to a lever, looking out over the crowd

with a slight, enigmatic smile on his face. He was well over six feet tall, thin to the point of emaciation, and had a bushy handlebar moustache over a scraggly goatee. Under his hat his eyes were dark as death and showed not the slightest trace of compassion for the men he was about to execute.

George Maledon, the executioner, also known as the Prince of Hangmen, bowed slightly as six men were led manacled up the steps to the platform and positioned next to the ropes.

The men ranged in age from early twenties to over forty, and all had their eyes on the ropes slowly swinging in what little breeze there was. Some of the faces showed resignation, some showed stark terror, and a couple mirrored the anger that had gotten them the sentence of death in the first place.

Maledon stepped to each man in turn and asked if they had any last words.

The first two merely shook their heads, eyes downcast and brimming with tears. One ignored Maledon, praying in a low, monotonous voice to the God he'd ignored his entire life until now. The fourth scowled and stared out at the crowd of spectators, grown suddenly quiet to hear what he had to say.

"I came here to get hanged, not to make no speech. Get on with it!"

The crowd cheered, some men waving hats and some ladies pumping their parasols up and down, urging Maledon to hurry up.

The fifth man mumbled a low, "I'm sorry for all the wrong I done," while the sixth just ignored the request for last words and stood there with eyes shut against the glare of the sun off the white paint, as if by not looking at the ropes he could forestall the inevitable end to his sorry life.

Maledon slowly put a hood over each man's head and positioned the hangman's noose, made with thirteen turns of the rope around itself so the knot would slide easily and break the neck at the second cervical vertebra, an injury that came to be known as a hangman's fracture.

Two of the men struggled against the hood, until a uniformed guard pinned their arms behind them and held them still until the hood and rope was in place.

"Easy now, boys," Maledon said in a low, gravelly voice over the sobs of the men who were crying softly, "you don't want to act the coward in front of all these good people."

When he was finished, Maledon stepped to his lever, pulled the safety pin out, and glanced at the county court building two hundred yards away. A dim figure could be seen in the second-floor window, watching the proceedings.

The figure, Judge Isaac Parker, hesitated for just

a moment before he nodded and turned away, letting the curtain fall to cover the window, sealing the fate of the men below.

Maledon pulled the lever and six souls were sent on their way to the hereafter, their bodies bouncing and jerking in a grotesque dance of death as each rope snapped with a sound like a rifleshot in the quiet morning air.

One man, who must have weighed over three hundred pounds, was beheaded by the sudden jerk as his body reached the limits of the rope in its six-foot drop. As the head hit the ground and rolled several feet, the body crumpled to the dirt, spewing a fountain of crimson blood in a high arc.

The crowd was stunned into silence at first, then cheered as some ladies and more than a few men bent over and vomited onto the dry grass.

After it was over and the bodies had been taken away to be buried in boot hill at the edge of town, the crowd began to disperse.

A man wearing a black-and-yellow checked suit came up to Maledon as he walked down the steps of the scaffold, holding a pad and pencil in his hand. He was followed by a younger man carrying a wooden camera on a tripod.

"Mr. Maledon, I'm Samuel J. Stevens from the *Post-Dispatch* newspaper. Would you answer a few questions for our readers?"

Maledon studied the man for a moment, then

glanced at the camera. He straightened his string tie and adjusted his hat to a slightly rakish angle. "Sure. Don't mind at all," he answered in his low, harsh voice.

"Aren't you worried that the ghosts of the men you hanged will come after you?" the reporter asked, his eyes drifting to the buckboard carrying bodies stacked like so much cordwood, as it winded its way toward the cemetery.

Maledon's lips curled in a small smile and the corners of his eyes crinkled, amused by the question. "Why, no I'm not," he answered. He pursed his lips as he, too, watched the bodies leaving. "I figure if I hanged the man, I hanged his ghost, too."

The reporter motioned to the photographer and Maledon put his hands on his coat lapels and stared into the camera, his eyes like black bullet holes in his face, his mouth a straight line of rectitude.

# Chapter 1

Alexandre Leo LeMat strolled before a row of oil paintings adorning his sitting room atop the Saint Anthony Hotel, critically examining his brush strokes, the finer points of portrait painting having been taught to him by his mentor George Catlin in Pennsylvania so many years ago. He paused in front of the painting of a beautiful woman with dark hair and piercing green eyes. "I miss you, my darling," he whispered to the likeness of his wife, his hand stretching out to gently touch the cheek on the canvas. He had painted the portrait from memory, since Angelique had died giving birth to their daughter, Angeline. Years had passed, yet the pain lingered. His years of training to become a physician had been useless. He was unable to save his wife, and the bitterness remained with him over time, causing him to leave the medical profession to follow other pursuits: painting . . . and offering his gun for hire.

Leo discovered early in life that he had an uncommon skill with a handgun, carrying his uncle's LeMat pistol in a shoulder holster, offering his services when occasion demanded. Quite often it was for money, other times simply a just cause. Growing up as first a boy, then a young man, in New Orleans, Leo had seen enough injustice to last him a lifetime. His mother, herself a distant relative of the Younger brothers, had instilled in him a feeling of compassion for the weak and defenseless, a passion he carried with him to this day.

His wanderlust took him all over the country. He had wealth from his family's vast fortune, most of which came from his uncle François's many weapon patents. Painting was Leo's passion, but a dark part of his nature kept him on edge, ready to use his gun at the slightest provocation. He often felt as if a demon lived inside him, occasionally rising to the surface, needing to be fed by violence.

Another portrait of a beautiful young girl caught his attention. His daughter's eyes seemed to fix on him. "I miss you, too, sweet Angeline," he said hoarsely, a lump in his throat. Angeline was attending a fancy boarding school back East, and though she often wrote Leo, he missed their long talks together.

He made ready to go to dinner with his associate, Jacques LeDieux. He'd spent too much time remembering old wounds. . . .

Alexandre Leo LeMat and Jacques LeDieux were having supper at the La Maison restaurant in San Antonio.

Jacques scowled down at his Boeuf Bourgundie, stirring the golden sauce with his fork. "The chef may speak with a French accent, my friend," he said, "but his food certainly does not."

Leo cut a piece of his roast beef au jus and dipped it in the sauce. He smiled. "I don't know what you're complaining about, Jacques. My food is excellent."

"How can you not know?" Jacques asked, his face becoming animated while engaging in his favorite pastime—complaining. "The meat is underdone, the sauce has too much garlic and not enough salt, and the potatoes . . ." He paused, spreading his hands. "Just let it be said they should have been left in the ground to rot rather than be treated with such indignity."

Leo took a sip of his Château Lafite. "Perhaps you just haven't had enough wine yet, *mon ami*, to enable you to enjoy our meal."

"There is not enough wine in San Antonio to make this food palatable," Jacques replied, pushing his plate away from him in disgust.

Leo was about to speak, when he was interrupted by a commotion at the table next to them. Two men, dressed as gentlemen in fine coats and high-necked collars, had just been served their soups. One of the men, a burly redhead with bushy, muttonchop sideburns and pink skin that was rapidly turning red and blotchy with anger, shouted at their waitress, "God damn it, this soup is awful!"

The waitress, a young woman barely out of her teens, her face paling at the violence of the man's reaction, said, "Yes, sir. I'm sorry. I'll bring you another kind."

The customer, slightly mollified, let her take the soup bowl away and began talking to his friend across the table in a loud voice, complaining about everything in the place from the service to the decor. As he talked and waved his arms around wildly, the man drank his wine in gulps instead of sipping it. A sure sign to Leo the man was without breeding.

Leo looked at Jacques. "Ah, a man after your own heart, Jacques. Perhaps you could join him at his table and compare notes on your critique of the cuisine of La Maison?"

Jacques glanced at the redhead, frowning. "No, I do not think so." He looked back at Leo. "I would rather eat the rest of this abominal food than sit with one so lacking in common courtesy."

Leo smiled. He was continually amazed at

Jacques's ability to read people. Though his associate had little formal schooling, Jacques was markedly intelligent and had an almost uncanny ability to judge someone's character. His judgments had proven to be accurate far more times than not.

"I am sure you're quite correct in your assumption, my friend. That man with the continual frown on his face is none other than Angus McGee, one of San Antonio's so-called gentlemen."

Jacques stared at McGee, not making any attempt to hide his displeasure at the man's mean-spirited countenance.

Leo continued with his description. "He is supposed to be of noble blood, but I find that hard to believe."

"He does appear to be wealthy." Jacques raised his eyebrows and grinned. "It is a shame mere wealth cannot buy good manners or breeding."

"He's quite wealthy. He made a fortune in land speculation . . . selling worthless prairie land to Easterners, greenhorns who didn't know better, through newspaper ads in New York and Chicago."

Leo went back to his dinner, determined not to let McGee's ill manners spoil his meal. He was finishing his roast beef when the waitress returned with their neighbor's soup. McGee tasted it, then scowled and threw his glass of water at the waitress, showering her with it as he yelled once again, "This is intolerable! I cannot eat this swill!"

Leo's patience with McGee's bad manners came to an end. He wiped his mouth with his linen napkin, winked at Jacques, then stood up and moved to the man's side. As McGee glanced up, Leo stuck his finger in McGee's soup and put it in his mouth. He smacked his lips and smiled. "Sir, could it be you are mistaken?" Leo said in a mild, gracious voice. "It doesn't taste so bad to me."

McGee's face turned blood-red as he jumped from his chair. "How dare you, sir?" he shouted, leaning forward to put his face near Leo's. "This is none of your affair, and I demand that you mind your own business."

Leo's voice remained mild and courteous, though his eyes grew hard and flat. "It *is* my business, when I come to eat at my favorite restaurant and find myself seated next to a rowdy oaf who is disturbing the entire establishment with his yelling."

McGee glared at Leo. "This food is uneatable," he spat.

Leo shrugged. "Perhaps that's because your taste in fine cuisine is as poor as your manners. I believe you owe the young woman waiting on you an apology. After all, she did not cook the food."

McGee's face blanched and he straightened,

pulling his coat down, squaring his shoulders. He casually picked up one of his driving gloves and gently slapped Leo across the face with it.

"I do not take such abuse from a stranger, sir. My second will contact you shortly."

Leo, keeping his face bland with the slightest hint of a smile, merely bowed and returned to his table.

Jacques grinned. "You see, my friend, I was right. A thoroughly disgusting character. So, now we fight another duel, eh?" he said.

Leo was unconcerned. "We'll see." He motioned the waitress over and ordered coffee for Jacques and himself.

A few minutes later, the man at the table with McGee approached Leo and handed him a card. "I am James Williams, and I am representing Mr. Angus McGee as his second in the duel," he said solemnly. "He wishes to know your preference in choice of weapons."

Leo pulled an elaborately engraved card out of his vest pocket. It read, DR. LEO LEMAT, PORTRAITIST, GUN FOR HIRE.

Williams's complexion darkened when he saw Leo's name.

"Jacques LeDieux here will be my second," Leo said. "And I choose pistols, of course."

"What?" the man said, almost strangling on the question.

Jacques answered, "You heard my principal. It is how duels are often fought among men of honor."

"I know who you are," Williams stammered. "Mr. McGee will never agree to face you. He does not know of your reputation."

Leo's eyes turned to the second. "Mr. McGee should know the rules of conduct before challenging someone to a duel. Now, you have my choice, and your principal can either take it or make a public apology to both me and the young lady," Leo said, his voice no longer mild. "Personally, I hope he chooses to fight."

Williams walked rapidly to the table and leaned over to talk to McGee, his voice low. There was no disguising the concern in his manner when he informed McGee of just whom he'd challenged to a duel.

Leo sipped his coffee, observing McGee out of the corner of his eyes. He could see McGee's face slacken when his second told him who Leo was. His face turned ever redder, a feat Leo would have said was impossible a moment before, and sweat began to form on his forehead. His mouth opened and closed, like a fish out of water too long, and his eyes darted around the room, as if looking to see who might be witness to his humiliation.

After a further whispered consultation with his second, McGee got ponderously to his feet and approached Leo, an expression on his face as if he'd just tasted something that came out of the south end of a cow.

With obvious embarrassment, he stuck out his hand. "Dr. LeMat, I misspoke earlier. I was wrong. Will you accept my apology?"

"Of course," Leo said, patting his lips with his linen napkin, not taking the outstretched hand or even glancing at the man. "As soon as you tell your young waitress you're sorry."

McGee drew himself up, and with as much dignity as he could manage, walked to the sideboard at the end of the room and bowed to the waitress he'd abused. Leo couldn't hear what was said, but the lady gave him a big smile as McGee walked out of the restaurant without looking back.

"Leo, I thought Monsieur McGee was going to die right on the spot," Jacques said. "His voice sounded like he was choking on his words."

"That was precisely the point," Leo replied. "I'm tired of dueling, and I'm tired of killing men who think they must fight to prove they are gentlemen. It's a custom that's outlived its usefulness."

"But it does seem to keep civility at a bare minimum when someone knows they may be killed for an impropriety."

"Perhaps." Leo leaned back in his chair and took a drink of his coffee chicory, and opened the San Antonio newspaper near his elbow.

Jacques leaned closer when he saw the picture on the front page. *"Mon Dieu,"* he muttered under his breath. It was a photo of five men hanging from a hangman's scaffold, with a tall, lean man dressed in black who looked like Death himself standing next to the hangman's lever. On the ground under the scaffold a headless body could be seen. The head was nowhere in sight.

"What is that?" Jacques asked, pointing at the headline, which read, HANGING JUDGE'S TOTAL OVER 150.

Leo glanced up from his reading. "It is a story of Federal Judge Isaac Parker. He has become known as the hanging judge because of the number of men he's sentenced to die."

Jacques shook his head. "He must have a heart of stone," he said.

"On the contrary," Leo remarked, "he is said to cry when he sentences men to hang, telling them it is the law killing them, not a personal thing."

"A poor argument to my way of thinking," Jacques replied. "That is like saying it is the bullet that has ended a man's life, not the man who pulled the trigger."

Leo's eyes narrowed. "But, all in all, a fascinating character," Leo muttered, as if to himself.

"Oh, no!" Jacques cried when he saw the light of interest in his friend's eyes. "Please, *mon ami*, do not tell me you are planning to travel to this"—Jacques leaned closer to read the name of the town again—"Fort Smith, Arkansas, to paint the judge's portrait."

"Judge Parker's jurisdiction is full of interesting subjects for my oils," Leo said, leaning back in his chair and raising his coffee cup to his lips. "Two of the judge's U.S. marshals, Heck Thomas and Bill Tilghman, have garnered national recognition for their efforts at policing the Indian Territory."

Jacques sighed. "And this Arkansas, it is hot, no?" he asked, a note of resignation in his voice.

"No hotter than San Antonio," Leo replied, a small smile curling the corners of his lips.

"That is like saying being shot is no worse than getting knifed. Neither is a welcome event," Jacques said. "So, I suppose I should begin packing and making the arrangements?"

Leo thought for a moment. "Yes. After all, the best thing to do during the summer in Texas . . . is to leave."

"I agree with that, Leo, but for once I wish you would be able to find suitable candidates for your portraits who lived in cooler areas, like Canada or perhaps the Dakotas, where the sun does not suck the life out of a man."

"But, Jacques, you know I prefer to paint men

of the West, men who live and die by their skill with a gun. Look at it this way," Leo continued, grinning broadly. "Perhaps you will find new recipes to add to your collection."

"Like what, *mon ami*? Armadillo, perhaps? The only things I've found worth eating west of the Mississippi are those that I myself prepare."

"Well," Leo said, finishing his coffee. "Maybe Arkansas will not be so hot as San Antonio."

"Hell itself is not so hot as San Antonio, Leo, but that does not mean I wish to visit there."

Jacques sighed, his shoulders moving with the effort. Though both he and Leo had been born and raised in New Orleans, itself no stranger to hot weather, that city at least had a steady cooling wind off the water to keep the temperature bearable. In San Antonio, where the wind, when it did blow, was as hot and dry as a Dutch oven's breath, Jacques always felt as if he were in danger of melting.

"I will see that our private coach is attached to the next Texas and Pacific train heading north," he said. He got up and started toward the door, adding over his shoulder, "And, since you insist on traveling to areas not known for their civility, I will also pack our usual supply of cartridges and ammunition for our weapons."

Leo laughed. "As the philosophers say, *mon ami*,

a short, full life is to be preferred over a long, dull one."

Jacques scowled. "And as my Cajun grandfather said, be careful what you wish for . . . you may get it."

"I believe it was the Chinese who said that," Leo said.

Jacques looked surprised. "If they did, they heard it first from him, for I am quite sure Grandfather spoke no Chinese."

# Chapter 2

While Jacques saw to the loading of their possessions into the baggage car of the Texas and Pacific train headed north to Fort Worth and then on to Fort Smith, Arkansas, Leo walked through their private coach, making sure no damage had been done while it was in storage.

Leo had been born into wealth and privilege, the nephew to the famous François LeMat, inventor of the LeMat pistol. His uncle had worked with General Beauregard of the Confederate Army during the Civil War to design and produce one of the most lethal weapons of its time, a pistol with a nine-shot cylinder that revolved around a .44-caliber barrel on top and a shorter 20-gauge shotgun barrel beneath. The pistols were in such demand they'd only been issued to Confederate officers and had made quite a name for themselves in the conflict between the states.

Leo's uncle had become rich beyond measure

from selling the guns after the war, along with other models he later invented. A confirmed bachelor, François had doted on his brother's wife and her son, Alexandre Leo LeMat, sharing both his home and his wealth after Leo's father was killed in a duel over a gambling debt.

Leo strolled through the coach, checking the expensive furniture for evidence of moths or rats, both of which tended to invade the car while stored.

He ran his hands over walls paneled in knotty pine, making sure they were polished to a gleaming luster. Satisfied all was in order, he stood in the middle of the car, hands on hips, glancing at the dark red Oriental rug covering the floor, the large settee against one wall with a mahogany table and two overstuffed Louis XIV chairs facing it, and the silver coffee service beside the sofa, reflecting golden light from the crystal chandelier overhead.

If one was forced to travel across desolate country unrelieved by beauty, it was certainly best to do so in the luxury of beautiful surroundings, he thought to himself.

Jacques entered, grumbling as usual about clumsy baggage handlers and inept stewards on the train. As Leo's constant companion since their childhood years, Jacques took it upon himself to see to the everyday necessities of their lives—the cooking, packing, overseeing servants, and such other things as their many travels required.

Since he'd been raised in abject poverty and had rarely set foot outside the city of New Orleans before meeting Leo, Jacques loved to travel and looked for almost any reason to convince Leo to undertake a journey to new places. The destination didn't matter nearly so much as the chance for Jacques to see country he'd never seen before. Short and squat where Leo was tall and lean, Jacques, in spite of the money he'd acquired working with Leo, still dressed as if ready for a day on the docks and wharves of New Orleans. Leo often accused Jacques of using his roughshod appearance to camouflage his innate intelligence, while Jacques countered it was often the best way to put people off their guard and to better judge their true character.

Leo, for his part, delighted in Jacques's appreciation of the fine books, music, and art he exposed him to, and Jacques responded by allowing Leo a chance to view the same things through another's eyes. It was an ideal friendship in almost every respect, despite vast differences in their cultural backgrounds.

Of course, Jacques never let his love of travel prevent him from complaining about every inch of the trip; it was just his way.

Jacques made his way to the rear of the coach

and began going through the cupboard, shaking his head in disgust. "I had a devil of a time finding vegetables and condiments fresh enough for my cooking, Leo," he said.

Leo smiled. Jacques was an excellent chef and never failed to provide cuisine fit for a king on their journeys. "I'm sure you will make whatever we have taste wonderful," Leo said.

"I will make us some coffee chicory before the train leaves," Jacques said, setting water to boil on the stove in the rear of the coach.

Leo settled on the couch and began studying various newspapers and magazines containing articles about Judge Isaac Parker. One issue of *Harper's* magazine contained a daguerreotype of the judge, showing him sitting, dressed in a dark coat with gold watch chain hanging from his vest. He was a distinguished-looking man, with short, dark hair parted on the left and a neatly trimmed moustache over a short goatee. Leo thought he looked almost patrician, with a long, straight nose and a high forehead indicating intelligence and poise.

As Jacques poured coffee into a china cup at Leo's elbow, Leo began making preliminary charcoal sketches from the picture, just to get a feel for the judge's visage. What began as random marks on the pad soon evolved into a remarkable likeness of Judge Parker. Jacques stood watching the portrait take shape. Even after all the years with Leo, he was still amazed at the way Leo could make his drawings come to life.

*"Mon ami,"* Jacques said, "I would give anything to have a tenth of your artistic talent."

Leo glanced up from his pad. "Oh, but you do, my friend," he said with a smile. "Only your art lies in your ability to make even the most mundane of foodstuffs taste as if they are fit for a king."

Jacques grinned and puffed out his chest at the compliment. *"Oui,* I guess it is true what my old grandfather used to say. The Lord gives to each of us some talent that makes us unique."

"Your grandfather was a wise man," Leo said, turning back to his drawing.

Jacques shrugged. "Wise enough to never leave the bayous where he was born to travel to lands suffocating in unbearable heat like his grandson."

By the time the train pulled into Fort Worth, after crossing hundreds of miles of land as flat and unexciting as a billiard table, with grass brown and sparse from the winter months, both Leo and Jacques were ready for a night or two in a fine hotel to break up the monotony of their journey.

As the train slowed with a hiss of steam from the brakes and a screeching of metal on metal from the wheels, Jacques leaned out the window to get his first glimpse of Fort Worth.

*"Mon Dieu!"* he exclaimed.

"What is it?" Leo asked from his place on the couch.

"The women here. They are beautiful!"

Leo laughed. "Any female would look beautiful to you after several days cooped up on a train, Jacques."

"Nevertheless," Jacques said, straightening his rumpled clothes, "I plan to make a much closer inspection this evening, after we find a hotel with a suitable bath tub."

Jacques had the coach put on a side-track so they could see the sights of the town. Jacques was especially interested in the area near the train station known as Hell's Half Acre, though it encompassed much more area than that.

Fort Worth was perhaps the most famous cowtown in Texas, and had more saloons, whorehouses, and gambling establishments than the entire rest of the state.

After checking into the Cattleman's Hotel, one

of the city's finest, home away from home to the state's richest cattle barons, Leo and Jacques took a walk down Main Street, finally ending up at the White Elephant Saloon.

The White Elephant was large, having room for not only many poker and faro tables, but also a stage for entertainers of all kinds and—they'd been told—a passable dining area.

Leo and Jacques took a table near the window, so Jacques could watch the hordes of people walking by on the wooden boardwalks that lined Main Street.

As he stared out the big double windows, Jacques said, "Leo, I have never seen so many people in one place at one time since Mardi Gras in New Orleans."

Leo nodded absentmindedly, his attention on a dapper-looking man seated at a nearby table. His face was vaguely familiar, and he felt he'd seen his picture someplace before.

Finally, after a few moments of reflection it came to him. He snapped his fingers and leaned over to whisper, "Look, Jacques. That man at the table next to us is Bat Masterson."

Jacques turned. "Who?"

"Bat Masterson," Leo replied. "One of the most famous men in the West. He's done it all, *mon ami.* He was an Army scout, buffalo hunter, gambler,

lawman, sportsman, and I hear he even writes oc-
casional articles for newspapers."

Jacques sighed. "Oh, now I remember. Wasn't
there something in one of your magazines about
him and a famous Indian battle?"

Leo smiled. "Yes, back in '74, I believe, he was a
member of a party of several dozen hunters who
fought off a large-scale Indian attack led by Quanah
Parker. The assault occurred at the hunters' head-
quarters at Adobe Walls in the Texas Panhandle,
but the professional sharpshooters, though greatly
outnumbered, repelled the Indians."

Jacques stared at the man, finding it hard to
believe a man dressed in a fine suit, wearing a
derby hat, and carrying a gold-headed cane could
have been so tough. "He does not look like an
Indian fighter to me." Jacques's nose wrinkled as
if he smelled something unripe. "He looks more
like a drummer or a dandy than a famous shootist."

"Looks can be deceiving, my friend, especially
in some of the Western gunfighters. After the battle at Adobe Walls, Masterson became an army
scout for General Nelson Miles for a while, then
opened a saloon in Dodge City, where he served
with his brother as city policeman before getting
elected sheriff of Ford County."

"Is he still sheriff there?" Jacques asked.

Leo shook his head. "No. He later became a deputy U.S. marshal and a hired detective for the Atchison, Topeka, and Santa Fe Railroad before fighting with Wyatt Earp and Luke Short in the Dodge City War."

Jacques glanced at Leo. "You seem to know quite a bit about this Bat Masterson."

"You know I have made a study of all the famous gunfighters of the West, Jacques, and Bat Masterson is one of the most famous."

As they spoke, another man joined Bat at his table. He was every bit as dapper as Bat, dressed in long, dark coat, full vest buttoned up to his neck, and wearing a top hat made of beaver. His tailored trousers had a bulge in the right front pocket, which to Leo's eyes looked like it contained a pistol, and there was a bulge under his left armpit that looked like a shoulder holster.

*For one dressed so fine, he's remarkably well armed,* Leo thought. Considerably smaller than Bat, Leo guessed him to be about five-foot-six and only a hundred and twenty-five pounds.

Jacques shook his head. "These men are all dressed as though they are attending an opera or a fine play. I have never seen such finery worn to a mere saloon." He glanced around the room. "Perhaps this Fort Worth is not so bad after all. We may even find a digestible meal here."

When their waiter appeared to take their orders, Leo asked, "Excuse me, but who is that gentleman sitting with Bat Masterson?"

The waiter turned his head, then looked back and smiled. "Why, that's Luke Short. He's part owner of the White Elephant with Jake Johnson."

After ordering beefsteaks, slightly charred, with mashed potatoes and green beans and a Caesar salad for two and a carafe of red wine, Leo looked at Jacques. "I can't believe my luck, to see both Bat Masterson and Luke Short in the same night."

"This Luke Short, he is as famous as Bat Masterson?" Jacques asked.

"Almost," Leo replied. "He was a house dealer at the Long Branch Saloon in Tombstone, Arizona, then joined Wyatt Earp and Doc Holliday at the Oriental Saloon. There they became fast friends and were known as the Dodge City Gang from their days in Kansas."

"Why don't you introduce yourself, Leo?" Jacques asked, taking a small sip of the wine to see if it was adequate or if it would have to be returned for a better vintage.

"I believe I will, as soon as we finish our meal," Leo replied.

Leo wiped his mouth with his napkin and started to get up to introduce himself to the next table, when a man approached the other table in a hurry. Leo sat back down to see what was happening before he intruded.

Luke Short looked up at the man. "Howdy, Jake. Have a drink?"

Jake Johnson shook his head. "No, ain't got time. That bastard Longhaired Jim Courtright is down the street, mouthin' off that he's gonna kill you if you don't keep your nose outta his business."

When Bat gave him a questioning look, Short explained, "Courtright has been asking Johnson here to pay him protection money to keep us from being robbed." Short shrugged. "So I told him to stick his protection up his butt."

Johnson looked at Bat. "Longhaired Jim says he's gonna tear the place up himself 'less we pay."

Bat smiled. "Well, gentlemen, let's go have a talk with this Longhaired Jim."

The three men got up from the table and walked out the batwings.

Leo threw some money on the table. "Come on, Jacques. This sounds interesting."

Jacques frowned, shaking his head. "I hate it when things get interesting. It always means gunplay."

They followed the three men to a nearby shooting gallery, and saw them approach a man watching patrons shoot at targets with .22-caliber rifles.

The man, obviously the Jim Courtright they'd

been speaking about, was wearing a Stetson hat and had a six-gun in a holster on his right hip, tied down low on his thigh in the manner of a gunfighter.

Short walked up to Courtright and said in a loud voice, "I hear you been shooting your mouth off about me, Jim."

Courtright turned and looked down at the shorter man, a sneer on his face. "Yeah, I think you oughta mind your own business, Short, an' keep your nose outta mine."

Short got right in the man's face. "Since I own a third interest in the White Elephant, it *is* my business, you bastard!"

Leo and Jacques were standing twenty feet away, and Jacques said, "Uh-oh, I believe you are right, *mon ami*, this *is* going to get interesting."

As he spoke, Short's right hand slipped inside his coat toward the bulge under his left armpit.

"Don't go for that gun, Short!" Courtright shouted, grabbing his six-gun from its holster and sticking the barrel against Short's chest.

Short shook his head. "I don't carry no pistol under my coat, Jim."

Courtright laughed and pulled the trigger. As the hammer on his Colt fell, it got caught in Short's watch chain and misfired.

Courtright's eyes widened. Short jerked a small

pistol from his shoulder holster and fired, the bullet shattering the cylinder on Courtright's Colt, sending it spinning from his hand.

Courtright took a step back, holding his hands out in front of him. "No, Luke . . . don't . . ."

Short began firing rapidly, emptying his pistol. Two shots went wild, but one of the other three hit Courtright in the right thumb, while another took him in the right shoulder and the last in the heart, knocking Courtright backward to land spread-eagled on his back in the dirt.

Leo, his physician's instincts coming to bear, rushed to the fallen man and examined him. Courtright stared up at Leo, a surprised look on his face, then his eyes clouded and stared into eternity.

Leo glanced up at Short, who was still standing with his smoking six-gun in his hand.

"He's dead," Leo said.

Short shrugged and holstered his pistol. "Good," he replied as he joined Masterson and Johnson, laughing and joking about the expression on Courtright's face when his gun jammed on Short's watch chain.

"It's a good thing he didn't ask you what time it was 'fore he tried to shoot," Johnson laughed.

"No, 'cause I would've told him it was time for him to take a dirt nap," Short replied.

Jacques stepped to Leo's side, shaking his head.

"*Mon Dieu*, but these men take a life as easily as I would swat a fly."

Leo stood up and looked around. The people standing nearby went back to their business without a further glance at the dead man lying on the street. There was no sign anywhere of a sheriff or marshal coming to investigate the shooting.

Leo shrugged. "Just another night in Fort Worth, I guess, Jacques."

Jacques inclined his head. "Come on, Leo. It must be about time for the floor show at the White Elephant to begin."

# Chapter 3

As Luke Short stalked off into the darkness with Jake Johnson, Bat Masterson hesitated, staring at Leo and Jacques with a questioning look on his face.

"I don't think I know you, mister," he said. "Are you new in town?"

Leo looked down at Longhaired Jim Courtright's cooling body, thinking what a savage town it was where when a man was killed the first question asked was whether someone standing nearby was new in town. He reached into his vest pocket and pulled out one of his cards and handed it to Bat with a short nod.

Bat held it up to the light from the nearby shooting gallery's lanterns and read, "Dr. Alexandre Leo LeMat, Portraitist, Gun for Hire."

He gave a short smile, looking at Leo over the card. "That's an interesting combination, Dr. LeMat."

Leo returned the grin. "And it often leads to an interesting life, Mr. Masterson. This is my friend and companion, Jacques LeDieux," Leo said.

When Bat nodded, Leo asked, "May we buy you a drink? There are some things I'd like to talk over with you."

Bat's smile widened into a full grin. "Well, Doc, I can't remember the last time I refused a free drink. Let's go."

As they walked away from the shooting gallery, he glanced sideways at Leo and Jacques. "Matter of fact, I can't remember the last time I refused a drink even when I had to pay for it."

At the White Elephant Saloon, Bat secured a table in a corner of the room and made a point of sitting with his back to a wall so he could have a view of the room and its occupants. Leo noticed his preoccupation with the seating arrangements and asked him about it.

"Do you always make it your practice to sit with your back to a wall, Mr. Masterson?"

Bat nodded. "Yeah, but call me Bat, Doc, everybody does."

"Is it because you have received threats against your life?" Jacques asked.

Bat made a hand signal to the barman, holding up three fingers, then he looked at Jacques. "Well, yes and no. I've not gotten any recent direct threats, Jacques, but I've been a lawman off and on for a number of years in some pretty rough places, and I've put quite a few men behind bars." He shrugged. "When they get out of a place like Yuma Territorial Prison, or the stockade at Fort Smith, they're often hankering to blame somebody else for their hard life. I just want to make sure if it's me they blame, I can see 'em coming when they try to get even."

After the waiter served them three glasses of whiskey, leaving the bottle on the table at Bat's request, Bat glanced at Leo with narrowed eyes, a speculative look on his face. "I know we've never met, Doc, but there's something awful familiar about your name and the fact that you're a painter who also hires his gun out." He drained half his glass in one quick motion of his head. "I can't quite put my finger on it, but it's there like an itch in the back of my head."

"Are you acquainted with Bill Hickok?" Leo asked. "We met with him and I painted his portrait a while back at his home in Kansas."

Bat nodded, but his expression was still puzzled. "Sure, I know Wild Bill. Everybody who's been out here longer a day and spent more'n an hour in a saloon knows Wild Bill, but I haven't spoken to him for a year or so. That's not it."

"Perhaps monsieur has heard about us from Wyatt Earp or Doc Holliday?" Jacques asked. "We also had some experiences with them recently."

Bat snapped his fingers. "That's it!" he said. "I talked with Wyatt and Doc when they were on their way through Colorado after that mess at the O.K. Corral last year. He mentioned something about a doctor and painter and gunman who'd helped him out. I didn't remember your name, only the fact of a painter and gunman being one and the same stuck in my mind."

"Is it so unusual for a man who is good with a gun to also be good at other things?" Leo asked, sipping his whiskey and trying to ignore the raw pain the cheap brand caused as it went down his throat.

"That's not what got me," Bat answered. "It was Doc Holliday saying he'd finally met a man as fast on the draw as he was."

Bat grinned and swallowed the rest of the whiskey in his glass in another quick drink. "And if you know Doc at all, that's quite an admission for him to make." He gave a short laugh. "Hell, he'd rather say someone had bested him with a woman than a gun."

Leo laughed. "Doc Holliday is quite a character. We enjoyed both his company and his humor very much on our visit to Tombstone."

Jacques smiled. "For one so close to death, both his and others', he seems to have an almost cheerful outlook on how he lives his life."

"Yeah, Doc always was as quick with his mouth

as he was with his six-gun," Bat said. "And what did you think of Big Nose Kate?"

"A remarkable woman," Leo said. "And very loyal to Doc."

"She wasn't with them when they came through Colorado, but I suspect she'll end up with Doc sooner or later . . . She always does," Bat observed.

Bat poured another round for the three of them, then he leaned back in his chair, sipping his drink this time as his eyes roamed the room, flicking back and forth quickly to check for danger.

"And what brings you and Jacques up to our neck of the woods, Doc?" he asked, finally satisfied there was no present danger in the saloon.

"As Wyatt may have told you, it is my . . . hobby to paint famous characters of the West, such as he and Bill Hickok and Doc Holliday. Jacques and I are on our way to Fort Smith to see if Judge Isaac Parker and perhaps Bill Tilghman or Heck Thomas will sit for me."

Bat laughed. "Well, old Bill and Heck are certainly famous, but as for Judge Parker, I'd say he was more *infamous*. Around here, he's known as the Hangin' Judge."

As Bat pulled a long, thin, black cigar from his pocket and lit it with a lucifer, Leo asked, "I've heard that, but I've also heard that the judge gets no pleasure from sentencing men to their death."

Bat blew a stream of blue smoke toward the

ceiling fans, where the wooden blades whirled the smoke into small clouds that soon mingled with the haze of cigarette and cigar smoke that permeated the room. "That's true, and I suppose it's not his fault that so many come to their death at the end of a rope. These are tough times for the territory, what with so many outlaws and bad men coming to the area to escape the law from other places." He gave a short grunt. "Hell, even most of the lawmen out here are on the run from crimes they've committed elsewhere. Who else would strap on a gun and risk their lives for less money than a cowpoke can make?"

"What are you doing here in Fort Worth, Bat?" Leo asked. "Are you planning on running for sheriff or deputy marshal again?"

Bat shook his head. "No, I think that part of my life is over. I'm getting on in years now and that's a game for a young man who has no thoughts of ever dying. Actually, right now, I'm making a pretty fair living teaching yokels the rudiments of the laws of chance as they pertain to poker."

"So, you are a gambler?" Jacques asked.

"With most of the people I play with, it ain't gambling," Bat said with a laugh. "But I'm getting kinda tired of it as a way of life. The hours stink, and so do the people you have to associate with. I think I'll try my hand at promoting some other things, like horse races and prizefights." He smiled. "That way, I get paid no matter who wins or loses."

"I've heard you also occasionally write articles for newspapers," Leo said.

"Yeah. It seems the people back East can't get enough to read about life out here on the 'frontier,'" Bat said. "So, of course, I gussy it up a little for the greenhorns and pilgrims who live in the big cities, make it seem a mite more exciting than it is." He hesitated. "Matter of fact, I've had an offer to move to New York and write full-time for *The Morning Telegraph*."

"Are you going to take them up on their offer?" Leo asked.

"Probably, but not just yet. I've still got a few good years out here left in me, so I'll hang around for a while and see what develops." He glanced around at the room full of rowdy, drinking men and women. "I figure life back East would be pretty tame after living out here. I'd probably be bored into an early grave."

Leo glanced at his watch. "Well, I must say it's been a great pleasure meeting and talking to someone as famous as you, Bat, but Jacques and I are due to leave on an early train for Fort Smith in the morning. I'm afraid we have to call it a night."

Bat leaned over the table and stuck his hand out. "Nice meeting you, Doc. You, too, Jacques.

But I do wish I'd been able to see you in action with that gun of yours. Doc Holliday said it was really something."

Leo stood up and took Bat's hand. "As you say, Bat, we're all getting older, and I hope I've left that behind me, too."

# Chapter 4

Bill Doolin's gang, known as the Wild Bunch, rode into the town of Ingalls for some rest and relaxation. They registered at the O.K. Hotel one at a time, adding their nicknames afterward: William Doolin (Bill), George Newcomb (Bitter Creek), Slaughter Kid, Tom Jones (Arkansas Tom), Dynamite Dick, Red Buck Waightman, and Tulsa Jack Starr. Bill Dalton, who was riding with them, elected to stay at his friend Bill Dunn's ranch two miles outside of town.

Deputy Marshal John Hixon was sitting in his office at Guthrie when he heard hooves beat a tattoo outside his door. He shifted in his chair so he could reach the pistol on his right hip and waited to see who was in such an all-fired hurry to see him.

A young man banged through the door, sweat beading his brow and staining his shirt from what appeared to be a long, hard ride.

"Marshal," the young man croaked through dry lips.

"Settle down, boy," Hixon said, inclining his head toward a coffee pot resting on a potbellied stove in the corner. "Why don't you wet your whistle 'fore you try an' talk?"

The boy grinned and stepped to the stove. "Thank you, sir," he said as he filled a stained, cracked cup on the nearby shelf. He drank it down, wiped the excess off his lips with the back of his hand, then turned to the marshal.

"Mr. Hixon, the deputy sheriff over at Ingalls sent me to get you."

Hixon paused in the building of a cigarette and glanced up at the boy. "Why's that, son?"

"He said to tell you the Wild Bunch just rode into town big as you please."

Hixon dropped his feet off the corner of his desk and sat up, dropping his cigarette makings in his surprise.

"The Wild Bunch? You sure, boy?"

"Yes, sir," the boy said, nodding his head vigorously. "The sheriff said to tell you they was all there, every one of them."

Hixon reached in his pocket and pulled out a fifty-cent piece. He flipped it to the boy. "Thanks, son. You go on over to the general store and get yourself an ice cream soda."

"Thank you!" the boy said and rushed from the room.

Hixon sat back in his chair, stroked his chin as he thought for a moment, then he grabbed his hat and walked out the door.

He stopped the first man he saw on the boardwalk. "George," he said, "head on over to the saloon and tell Marshal Thomas to come see me at my office as soon as he can, will ya'?"

"Sure, Marshal," George said and hurried down the street.

Hixon went back into his office, took a bottle of whiskey out of his right-hand desk drawer, and poured a generous jolt into his coffee cup. He sipped it as he waited for Heck Thomas to come.

"Heck, I hear Bill Doolin an' his gang are holed up over at Ingalls," John Hixon said as he poured Thomas a couple of inches of whiskey into a tall glass on his desk. "I got an idea how we can get 'em."

Heck Thomas sat across from Hixon's desk and smoked a cigarette, crossing his long lanky legs and leaning back in the straight-backed chair. "Go on," he said, tilting smoke from his nostrils as he picked up the glass and took a drink.

"Since they announced the opening of the Outlet, homesteaders have been comin' in here by the droves. I figure if we get a couple of covered wagons an' fill 'em up with deputies, we could get right down into the middle of town 'fore those bandits knew what hit 'em."

Heck frowned through the cloud of cigarette smoke hanging in the still air around his head. "Just how many deputies you planning on taking along?"

Hixon thought for a moment, counting figures in his head. "I know 'bout twelve or thirteen men I can get on short notice. That oughta be enough. We can send one wagon in from Guthrie an' one from Stillwater. That way the bandits won't suspect nothin'."

"I don't know, John," Thomas said, finishing off the whiskey without removing the cigarette from his lips. "I've been chasing outlaws for a lotta years and I make it my practice to never go into a situation like that with more than two or three men. You go into Ingalls with a whole passel of men armed to the teeth and loaded for bear, you're gonna bring a lotta bodies out . . . and not all of 'em are gonna be outlaws. Sun's gonna be down 'fore you can get the men together and get over there. Fighting like that in the dark against desperate men, your men are gonna be shooting each other as much as the Doolin Gang are."

Hixon tried to press his point. "But, Heck, this

is the first time we've managed to get a line on 'em where they's all gathered together in one place, an' they don't know we know it."

Heck nodded, not willing to be pushed into an act he thought foolhardy. "I know, John. Why don't you let me take Detective Dodge and one other man over there in the morning? I guarantee you we'll bring 'em in."

Hixon bowed his back. "No, by damn! This is my jurisdiction an' I say we go in tonight, an' go in strong."

Heck shook his head. "If you go in with that many men, you're going in without me."

Hixon stood up, his face and neck red with anger. "So be it, then! You an' Dodge can stay here an' cool your heels in Guthrie. I'll take my boys an' bring in the Doolin Gang."

Heck Thomas got slowly to his feet. "Thanks for the whiskey, John, and I wish you'd take my advice."

Hixon bit his lip to keep from telling Thomas what he could do with his advice.

As the wagons approached Ingalls from Guthrie and Stillwater, Hixon sent a scout named Red Lucas into town posing as a fisherman from Bear Creek. He reported back the Wild Bunch was staying at the O.K. Hotel and their horses were at Ransom's Livery Stable.

The wagon from Stillwater, containing Tom Hueston, Dick Speed, Ham Hueston, Henry Keller, M.A. Iauson, Hi Thompson, and George Cox arrived on time on the outskirts of Ingalls. The wagon from Guthrie, led by Deputy Marshal John Hixon and holding Jim Masterson, Doc Roberts, Ike Steel, Steve Burke, and Lafe Shadley was delayed and didn't make the rendezvous until almost midnight.

Red Lucas snuck back into town and found Doolin, Dalton, Newcomb, Red Buck Waightman, Dynamite Dick, and Tulsa Jack in Ransom's Saloon drinking and playing poker.

Hixon and his group finally arrived, and Hixon scattered his men along the south side of town to cut off any avenue of escape.

The other wagon's occupants, all carrying rifles and pistols, hid silently behind brush, fences, and buildings along the west side of town.

In Ransom's Saloon, Bitter Creek Newcomb was busted, having bet his load on a pair of aces and been beaten by three deuces. He decided to go for a walk and have a cigarette.

As he stepped into the narrow street, he saw the wagons enter town and stop in the darkness at the end of the road. *Hell,* he thought as he put a match to his cigarette. *Wonder what those wagons're doin' down there in the middle of the night?*

He climbed on his horse and began to walk it

down the street, hoping the fresh night air would clear some of the whiskey from his head.

Dick Speed ran bent over holding his Winchester close to his chest into the Pierce and Hostetter Feed Barn. Two young men sweeping the floor looked up in fright at the sight of an armed man rushing in the door, sweat pouring from his face.

"Get your hands up an' stand over there," Speed said, pointing his rifle at the boys. "I'm a federal officer here to arrest the Wild Bunch, an' if you make a move to warn 'em, I'll kill you dead."

Speed eased back to the doorway and looked out down the street. When he saw a man riding his way, he levered a shell into the firing chamber of the rifle and flattened himself against the wall.

Dell Simmons, a nineteen-year-old, stepped out of Light's Blacksmith Shop across the street. Speed called to him in a low whisper, "Hey, boy. Come here a minute."

Dell walked over, his hands in his pockets. "Yeah, whatta you want?"

"Who's that man on the horse over yonder?" Speed asked.

Dell took a look. "Why, that's Bitter Creek," he said.

Bitter Creek Newcomb saw the boy pointing at him as he talked to a dark figure in the doorway. Years riding the owl hoot trail had taught him to be cautious. He leaned over and grabbed his rifle from his saddle boot just in case there was to be trouble.

Speed threw his rifle to his shoulder, took quick aim, and fired. His slug slammed into the magazine of Bitter Creek's rifle, ricocheted downward, and tore into the outlaw's right leg.

Newcomb flinched as he returned fire, missing Speed. Unable to lever another cartridge into his broken rifle, he wheeled his horse and put the spurs to it.

Speed swung from the doorway and took dead aim at the man's back.

Arkansas Tom, half asleep on the top floor of the O.K. Hotel, jumped up at the first sound of gunfire, grabbed his rifle, and leaned out the window.

He saw Deputy Speed aiming his rifle at Bitter Creek's back, and fired, hitting him in the shoulder.

Speed was twisted half around by the force of the slug, but tried to make it to his wagon. Just before he reached cover, crawling on his hands and knees, Arkansas Tom fired again. His slug split the space between Speed's shoulder blades, killing him instantly.

"God damn it!" Deputy Marshal Hixon yelled when he heard the gunshots. His men weren't in position yet.

As Bitter Creek rode south down the street, bent over his saddle horn holding his useless rifle in his right hand, Hixon's men stood up and began shooting at him as he sped by.

Doolin, Dalton, Tulsa Jack, Dynamite Dick, and Red Buck ran to the windows of Ransom's Saloon, broke the glass out and began firing their pistols to cover his escape.

Hot lead slugs filled the night air and clouds of gunsmoke poured from the saloon as if it were on fire. Flashes of light split the night like lightning as flame belched from gun barrels.

A wild shot struck Dell Simmons in the chest, mortally wounding the nineteen-year-old. One of the other customers in Ransom's Saloon, wanting no part of a gunfight, burst out the door, holding his hands high. Two of Hixon's men, thinking he was one of the outlaws, opened fire, shooting him through the liver.

Bitter Creek, slugs flying around his head like angry bees, managed to make it to thick timber at the edge of town.

The firing stopped. Hueston and his men used the break to move closer to the saloon on the west side of Ash Street, while Hixon's men eased through brush east of the hotel so they could cover both the front of the saloon and Ransom's Livery Stable where the outlaws kept their horses.

Hixon cupped his hands around his mouth and

shouted, "Come on out, Doolin! You men are surrounded. You got no chance to escape."

Doolin hollered back out the window, "Go to
hell!" He ducked back just as the marshals all
opened fire again, sending a withering barrage of
bullets into the saloon, the slugs tearing into the
front, side, and rear of the wooden building.

Ransom, hunkered down behind the bar,
screamed as a bullet tore into his leg, and Doolin
shouted at his men, "Come on, boys. Make a run
for the hosses!"

Doolin led Dalton, Red Buck, Dynamite Dick,
and Tulsa Jack out the side door of the saloon
toward the livery.

Murray, to give them cover, opened the front
door of the saloon and stuck his rifle out. Three
of the deputies fired simultaneously. Two shots
struck him in the ribs and one broke his arm. He
was thrown back inside, his Winchester falling in
the doorway.

As the outlaws gained the livery and began firing at the deputies, it forced Hueston's men to
shift positions to cover the stables. Hueston slipped
behind a pile of lumber and took aim at the rear
door of the livery.

Arkansas Tom, on the top floor of the hotel,
stood on a chair to get a better look at the fight
below. From this vantage point, he could just see
the outline of Deputy Hueston as he aimed his

rifle over the lumber. He fired three quick shots, taking Hueston twice in the left side and once in the gut.

Inside the barn, Doolin and Dynamite Dick quickly saddled horses while Dalton, Red Buck, and Tulsa Jack pumped rapid, accurate fire at Hixon's men from the doorway.

"Come on, boys," Doolin said when the horses were ready. He and Dynamite Dick swung into their saddles and made a wild dash out the rear door to the southwest. Dalton, Red Buck, and Tulsa Jack rode out the front door, leaning over their saddle horns and firing to either side as they headed for a ravine a few hundred yards away.

As Dalton rode hell-bent for leather down the street, Deputy Hixon stood up from behind a barrel and fired, hitting Dalton's horse in the jaw. The horse screamed and bucked and crow-hopped, almost unseating Dalton, until he finally got it under control and running again.

Deputy Shadley fired, hitting the animal in its leg, breaking it and knocking Dalton from the saddle. Dalton grabbed the reins and saddle horn and moved beside the limping, bleeding animal, using it for cover. Shadley fired again, pocking dirt at Dalton's feet, causing him to abandon the wounded horse and dive over an embankment into high grass.

Dalton peeked up out of the grass and saw his

friends stopped by a wire fence, trapped and unable to proceed. He remembered he had a pair of wire cutters in his saddlebags and jumped up out of the grass and headed back toward his horse.

Shadley, seeing his chance to take Dalton out, jumped from his cover and ran toward Dalton. He came to a yard fence and tried to run through it, but his coat caught, throwing him forward onto his stomach.

Arkansas Tom took dead aim from the hotel and fired, his bullet striking Shadley in the right hip, shattering the bone and lodging in his right breast. Shadley managed to untangle himself from the fence and crawled to the Ransom house, where he banged on the door and yelled for help.

Peeking from behind a window curtain, Mrs. Ransom shook her head. "No, you get the hell outta here! If you want help, go on over to that cave over yonder," she said, pointing across the street. "There's a doctor there."

Shadley, unable to walk on his shattered hip, began to crawl across the street, when several more shots rang out, all hitting the wounded deputy in the back.

Dalton grabbed the wire cutters from his saddlebags, shot his horse in the head, and headed back to the fence where his partners were trapped.

Jim Masterson began firing on the men from behind a blackjack tree a few dozen yards away.

Dalton's men opened fire, almost cutting the thin tree in half. Masterson soon ran out of ammunition and made a dash through heavy fire to his wagon, where he filled his pockets with cartridges and then ran back to the tree.

While Masterson was reloading, Dalton cut the wires and let the gang ride through. They came up out of the gully on horseback, whipping their horses to get more speed.

"Hell, fellers, they're gettin' away!" Masterson shouted, stepping out from behind the tree and opening fire, accompanied by Hixon, Roberts, Steel, and Burke.

Dynamite Dick was blown off his horse, but the outlaws paused long enough to lift him back in the saddle and take off again.

By now the outlaws were almost out of sight, so Masterson raised the sights on his Winchester to five hundred yards and fired one last time, but they were out of range.

"They're gone," Masterson said, lowering his rifle.

"God damn it," Hixon shouted, "there's still some of 'em left in the hotel. That's where the shots came from that got Speed an' Hueston an' Shadley."

Hixon gathered his men and hurried to the hotel. "Everybody come on out," Hixon shouted.

All of the occupants of the hotel exited except

Arkansas Tom. When he refused to leave, the deputies all began firing into the upper floor of the building, peppering it with hundreds of bullet holes.

For over an hour they fired, receiving fire back from Arkansas Tom the whole time.

Finally, Hixon shouted, "Come on out! You can't get away."

"If I come out, I'll come shootin'," Arkansas Tom shouted back.

Masterson walked to the south side of the building and put dynamite sticks against the wall. "If you don't come out, we'll blow the damn building to pieces!" he shouted.

"Blow away and be damned with you!" Arkansas Tom responded, firing a round out the window to punctuate his words.

As Masterson bent down with a match in his hand, a man came up and grabbed him by the shoulder. "Hold on a minute, mister," the man pleaded. "This here's my hotel. Let me try an' talk some sense into that boy 'fore you blow it up."

Masterson nodded and the man eased into the back door of the hotel, calling out to Arkansas Tom he was coming up unarmed to talk.

Some time later, after the owner of the hotel begged him to come out and not let them destroy his hotel, Arkansas Tom surrendered.

He was taken to the Payne County Jail.

Deputies Speed, Hueston, and Shadley all died of their wounds.

Bitter Creek Newcomb left a blood trail across half of the state, but he recovered from his wounds and was not captured.

Heck Thomas had been right. There were plenty of bodies on both sides.

# Chapter 5

Leo and Jacques checked into the Star Hotel in Fort Smith and had the desk clerk send a couple of boys to get their baggage from the railroad station.

"Monsieur," Jacques said, leaning his elbow on the desk and addressing the clerk, "could you direct us to the nearest restaurant that might have food fit to eat?"

"Why," the man said, scratching his chin as if he had to think about it for a moment, "I guess the best place in town is Bea's Boarding House, over on sixth street."

"You are sending us to a boarding house?" Jacques asked.

"That's if you want real meat-and-potatoes type food 'stead of that fancy crap with names you can't even pronounce they serve over at the Florentine."

Jacques looked at Leo and shook his head.

"Would the Florentine perhaps be a French restaurant?" Jacques asked.

He nodded. "Yeah, but you don't want to go there, mister. They cover the food with all kinds of weird sauces an' stuff till you can't even taste the meat."

Jacques said, "Thank you kindly," to the clerk and he and Leo walked out onto the boardwalk, both trying to keep from laughing.

As they walked, Jacques glanced at the men and women strolling along the boardwalks with them. "It would seem the typical cuisine in this town is as lacking in culture as the women seem to be lacking in beauty," Jacques observed, noticing the rather plain dress of both the men and women around them.

Leo shook his head. "Don't be such a snob, Jacques," he said. "These are plain folk of the West, and for the most part they have no use for fine dresses and suits. Their clothing is made for comfort and to wear well, not for impressing visitors from the high society of New Orleans such as yourself."

Jacques assumed a wry smile. "Do I really sound like a snob, *mon ami*?"

Leo nodded. "I can remember when you only had one pair of trousers to wear, my friend, and you only washed them once a week, whether they needed it or not," Leo said pointedly.

"That was long before you introduced me to the finer things in life, Leo, such as women who bathed for the fun of it, not out of necessity."

The hour was early, just before noon, and neither man was in a great hurry to eat.

"How about we walk around the town, my friend," Leo said, "and try to get a feel for the flavor of this place."

Jacques glanced back at the hotel. "If the cleverness of that desk clerk is any indication, the flavor of Fort Smith will be very bland."

Leo spied a number of shops and stores to the left toward the center of town. As they were passing a storefront with a sign proclaiming it to be Madame Laury's Dress Shop, the front door opened and a young lady carrying several boxes came rushing out.

The boxes were piled so high she couldn't see Jacques and she barreled into him, knocking both of them sprawling into the street.

*"Mon Dieu,"* Jacques shouted as he tumbled end over end onto the dirt.

The young woman landed facedown in a small patch of mud where a horse had recently relieved himself. She rolled over and sat up, her legs outstretched in front of her. "Oh . . . Oh, my goodness!" she cried. "Look what you've done to my dress!" She stared at Jacques as if he had dumped her in the mud on purpose.

Leo, at first mildly amused by the incident, suddenly stopped as he took a good look at the woman. She had long, dark hair hanging in gentle curls down around her shoulders. Her eyes were sea green, and her face was thin with high cheekbones and a patrician nose. She was beautiful. And, Leo thought, she so closely resembled his wife she could have been her sister.

With dry mouth and pounding heart, Leo shook his head to clear his thoughts and stepped from the boardwalk.

"Here, miss, let me help you up," he said, bending over to reach for her.

She glared up at him and pushed his hand away. "I don't need your help," she spat. She rolled to the side and climbed to her feet, using a hitching rail to pull herself up.

Jacques jumped nimbly erect and dusted himself off, looking at the young lady as if afraid she might once again attack him.

"Jacques," Leo said, "help the young woman pick up her packages."

Jacques gave Leo a look, but helped him gather the packages and boxes the lady had been carrying.

As Leo handed them to her, he touched his hat and bowed slightly. "I am Leo LeMat, and this is my friend Jacques LeDieux." He noticed the girl was tall, coming almost up to his chin, and she was slim, with curves filling out her dress in all the right places.

The girl stared angrily at him for a moment, and then she began to laugh. It was a low, full, throaty laugh, not the dainty high-pitched sound that young women usually affect. It made Leo want to smile and laugh out loud with her. She was having quite an effect on him.

"Hello," she said. "My name's Margaret Cartwright, but everyone calls me Maggie."

Leo gave another short bow. "I shall call you Margaret," he said.

Her eyes focused on Leo for a few seconds and the smile faded from her lips as she regarded him intently. She seemed to shiver, then broke her gaze and walked hurriedly up the street, calling back, "Good day, gentlemen."

As she walked away, Leo stared after her. "Jacques," he said, "I think I'm in love."

His friend looked at him. *"Mais ça c'est fou!"* he whispered fiercely.

Leo shook his head. "No, it's not crazy. Something about her touched my heart just now."

He glanced sideways at Jacques as they began to walk down the boardwalk. "Didn't you notice how much she looked like my Angelique?"

Jacques looked sadly at Leo, thinking back on how his friend had been almost killed by the terrible blow of his wife dying in childbirth while giving birth to his daughter, Angeline. Had it not been for the responsibility of caring for his new young child, Jacques felt Leo would have gone insane with grief.

*"Oui, mon ami,"* Jacques replied in a low voice, "she does indeed resemble both Angelique and Angeline."

Leo turned, smiling, his somber mood of moments before broken. "Oh, she is not nearly so beautiful as my darling daughter . . . but she is close, Jacques, she is very close."

Jacques nodded, relieved. Sometimes the mere mention of his daughter's name, who was away attending a boarding school for young ladies of distinction in New Orleans, would send Leo into a fit of depression for days and make him melancholy and almost unbearable to be around.

"And do you intend to pursue this young vision of beauty, Leo?" Jacques said, a teasing tone in his voice.

"Not on the basis of one chance encounter, Jacques. We shall have to see what fate has in mind for us. If I am intended to see more of Miss Cartwright, then our paths will cross again."

"Good," Jacques said, rubbing his stomach. "Enough of this idle chatter. Let us find a suitable restaurant soon, for I am so hungry my stomach thinks my throat has been cut."

Jacques pushed himself back from the table, a satisfied look on his face as he took his linen napkin and wiped his lips.

"I take it from your expression and the sounds you made as you wolfed your food down that your meal was satisfactory?" Leo asked.

"*Oui*. The Florentine is a small oasis of civility in this bastion of mediocrity known as Fort Smith."

"I agree," Leo said. "The food was as good as any we used to have in New Orleans."

"I wouldn't go *that* far, my friend, but it was certainly adequate."

Leo put some bills on the table and stood up. "Good. Then let us proceed to the court building. The afternoon session should be starting soon and I'd like to see Judge Parker in action."

It was a short walk from the Florentine to the federal courthouse where Judge Isaac Parker held court.

Leo and Jacques stopped a moment in front of the building to admire its clean, functional appearance. Three stories high with a multitude of windows on each floor and bright whitewashed wooden walls with brick veneer on the lower floors, it was an imposing thing in a town like Fort Smith, where most of the buildings were made of wood and were only one or two stories tall at the most.

As they walked to the entrance, Jacques noticed something through the small windows almost at ground level. He moved off the gravel path and bent over, peering inside.

"Leo, come here," he called quietly.

Leo glanced around and saw none of the passersby were paying them any attention so he went to Jacques's side and looked in the windows.

Just below the ground was a small, dark, dirt-floored room that encompassed the entire length and breadth of the courthouse. All along the walls were chains and manacles bolted in place, hanging unused and rusting among the cobwebs of the room.

"*Mon Dieu,* Leo," Jacques whispered, though there was no one about to hear them. "It is like a dungeon."

Leo nodded, his face thoughtful. "That's exactly what it is . . . or *was*, my friend. Evidently, the judge has recently made other arrangements for the prisoners."

Jacques shivered as he looked in at the dark room. "I can almost believe a prisoner confined in there would look forward to the hanging, if only as an escape from the darkness of this terrible place."

"Come, Jacques," Leo said softly, placing his hand on his friend's shoulder and breaking the spell of the dungeon. "Let's go see what Judge Parker has in store for us today."

They climbed three flights of mahogany stairs to the judge's courtroom on the third floor and entered. The room was about sixty feet long by forty feet wide, with a tall desk at one end made of some sort of black wood with ornate figures carved into it on all sides. The desk was up on a platform and thus the top was level with a man's neck, so when Judge Parker sat in his high-backed leather chair, everyone would have to look up at him.

Arrayed in front of the judge's desk were two tables, one on his right and one on his left. At the one on his right sat the defendants and their lawyers. The prosecuting authorities sat at the desk on the judge's left.

Next to the judge's desk was a single chair with a small rail around it where witnesses sat while being questioned, either by the attorneys or the judge himself.

Behind the attorneys' tables was another rail, behind which were arrayed in neat order forty straight-backed wooden chairs for visitors or family members of the accused.

When Leo and Jacques entered, a guard standing to the side of the door leaned over and whispered,

"No guns allowed. If you're heeled, hang 'em on the wall." He inclined his head toward a row of pegs on the wall, some of which had holsters and gun belts hanging.

Leo hesitated. Out of long habit, he never went anywhere without carrying his Baby LeMat pistol in his shoulder holster. But, he thought, if he wanted to paint Judge Parker's portrait, he'd better not start by disobeying the judge's rules in his own courtroom. He withdrew his pistol and placed it on a table under the pegs, noticing the guard's eyes widen at the sight of the unique gun.

The guard's eyes widened further when Jacques pulled not only a pistol from his belt but also his twelve-inch Bowie knife from a boot scabbard and laid them next to Leo's LeMat.

Leo and Jacques proceeded up the aisle and took seats near the front of the courtroom. There were only a few other people present, indicating that it was to be a slow day.

Three men were led in by a deputy and made to sit at the defendants' table. They were all wearing manacles on their ankles so they had to take small, shuffling steps lest they trip. One had a large bruise under his left eye and another had his right hand bandaged, his arm in a sling.

From a door across the room, a tall man with thinning hair and a large, bushy moustache covering his entire upper lip slowly entered. He had a badge on his vest made up of a star with a half-moon over it. When he looked at the defendants, they all dropped their gaze, unwilling to look him in the eye.

Leo leaned over and whispered, "That must be one of Judge Parker's deputy marshals."

The marshal took a seat next to a man sitting at the prosecutor's table.

Minutes later, the door at the front of the room opened and Judge Isaac Parker entered. A man of only medium height and build, he nevertheless carried himself with an almost regal bearing and had a stern look on his face. Leo thought he would certainly hate to be one of the men sitting at the table about to be judged.

Parker took his seat behind his desk, donned a pair of glasses, picked up a gavel, and gave a short rap on his desk. "Federal Court in the District of Oklahoma Territory is now in session," he said gravely.

He looked at a sheaf of papers on the desk and read, "William Brody, Joshua Pickens, and Thomas Beckett, you have been charged with assault on a deputy U.S. marshal and endangering the life of a district judge. How do you plead?"

A man in an ill-fitting suit sitting next to the three men stood up. He had slicked-back hair glistening with an abundance of pomade and a pencil-thin moustache, which curled up at the corners. He looked more like a drummer selling whiskey than an attorney.

"My clients plead not guilty, Your Honor," he said.

Parker raised his eyebrows slightly, as if to say he doubted anyone in his court could be innocent.

"Mr. Prosecutor, call your first witness," the judge intoned in a low, hard voice.

The man at the table with the marshal got up, and the marshal got slowly to his feet and walked to the witness stand. After being sworn in by a bailiff, he took his seat.

The prosecutor said, "State your name please."

"I'm U.S. Marshal Chris Madsen," the marshal said in a bored voice, as if he'd done this many times before.

"Please tell the court the circumstances of your arrest of the defendants."

"I was on duty escorting District Judge Wallace Bream to Beaver City, Oklahoma. Judge Bream and I bedded down in a room over a saloon, all the hotels being full at the time. 'Long 'bout midnight, some drunks in the saloon below began discharging their firearms."

"And what happened then, Marshal Madsen?" the prosecutor asked, strolling back and forth in front of the witness stand, his thumbs hooked in his vest.

"I didn't do nothin' at first, that not bein' too

unusual for Beaver City, till the slugs started comin' through the floor of our room an' endangerin' the life of the judge."

The prosecutor stopped his pacing and raised his eyebrows in surprise, though it was evident he knew exactly what the marshal was going to say. "And then what did you do?" he asked, glancing out of the corner of his eye at the judge to make sure he was listening.

"I proceeded downstairs to ask the gentlemen to stop their shootin'."

"And what did you find?"

The marshal pointed to the man called Brody. "Mr. Brody there had a six-shooter in his hand an' was in the process of firin' it willy-nilly all over the place. I jerked it outta his hand and prepared to go back to bed."

"And then what happened?"

"Mr. Pickens there jumped in my face and said, 'I'm a son of a bitch from Cripple Creek.' " Marshal Madsen almost smiled. "I told him I knew *what* he was, I just didn't know where he was from."

Several of the spectators laughed out loud at the marshal's description of the conversation, until Judge Parker banged his gavel, his face somber. Leo thought he'd never seen a man so devoid of a sense of humor.

"Then Pickens took a swing at me, so I clubbed him to the floor with the gun I took from Brody,"

Madsen continued, still speaking in a bored tone of voice, as if the action of taking a gun from a man and clubbing another over the head with it was an everyday part of his job.

"Is that how the defendant got his black eye?" the prosecuting attorney asked, turning to glance at the defendant.

Madsen spread his palms, as if the fact was self-evident.

"After that, Mr. Beckett over there pulled his gun on me, but I shot first, wingin' him in his shootin' hand." Madsen leaned back. "Then I took them all into custody."

"That's all the questions I have, Your Honor," the prosecutor said, returning to his table.

The lawyer for the defense stood up. "Marshal Madsen, isn't it true my clients were just doing what most men do in Beaver City after dark? Just out having a good time without meaning to harm anyone?"

The marshal hesitated, then he grinned and said, "Yeah, I suppose so. It's a pretty rowdy town, all right."

"Did you identify yourself as a U.S. marshal to Mr. Brody before you took his pistol from him?"

Madsen shook his head. "Nope." He pointed at the badge on his vest. "But this here badge is kinda hard to miss, especially when I'm standin' right in front of you."

The lawyer smiled broadly. "I have no further questions for the marshal," he said.

After Madsen got to his feet and walked slowly back to his seat, the lawyer said, "Your Honor, my clients were just men out doing what men do, celebrating a little. They had no idea the marshal was a lawman, so I ask that the charges against them be dismissed."

Parker hesitated, looking over his half-glasses at the three men sitting at the table in front of him.

"Sir, I take it that your clients were not only drunk, they were *blind* drunk to have missed the badge on Mr. Madsen's chest, which I can quite plainly see from this distance of twenty feet."

The lawyer's face turned red and he stuttered, "But . . . Your Honor . . ."

"I will take into account the fact that no harm was done to anyone by your clients, thanks in large part to the quick thinking and actions of Marshal Madsen," Parker interrupted, "so I will be lenient with them. Thirty days and thirty dollars each," he said, banging his gavel down with finality.

As the judge bent over his desk to write his verdict in the file in front of him, Leo leaned over to whisper to Jacques, "From what I've heard about this judge, I'm surprised he did not give them a harsher sentence."

Jacques looked at him. "Thirty days in the jail

we saw downstairs would be almost as bad as hanging, my friend, and thirty dollars is probably two months' wage for those fellows. That is not so easy a sentence I think."

"It is when you think they could easily have been shot by the marshal for drawing a gun on him," Leo said, smiling.

# Chapter 6

Margaret Cartwright could not believe her ears. She had entered the courtroom in time to hear all of the testimony about the three men Marshal Madsen brought in, and was astounded at the lightness of the sentence handed down by Judge Parker.

Unable to contain herself any longer, she jumped to her feet and approached the bench. "Judge Parker," she said in a loud, authoritative voice, "might I be heard?"

Parker looked up from the pile of papers he was reading, and she thought she could see the resignation in his eyes when he saw her. They'd crossed swords before, and she knew her persistence in her ideals bothered the judge.

"Ah, Miss Cartwright," he intoned in a voice devoid of friendliness. "Since you've arrived in Fort Smith I've rarely been able to keep you from being heard, so I suppose today will be no different. You may speak, but please, no sermons. Keep it brief."

"Yes, sir. I feel it is my duty as a citizen of the state to protest the mild sentence you've handed down today. These . . . men," she said, glancing at the defendants' table, scorn dripping from her voice, "have perpetrated a most grievous assault on an officer of this court, and they did it while under the influence of demon rum. A sentence as you've handed down today amounts to no more than a wink and a shrug at men who would partake of the devil's brew and then commit havoc on innocent citizens. I feel a much more severe judgment is necessary to help to convince other men of the dangers of engaging in such ruinous behavior."

She was just getting started when Parker held up his hand. "Miss Cartwright, please! I asked you to be brief and to refrain from giving one of your usual sermons."

"I have just a few more comments. . . ."

"No," Parker said, wagging his head, "you've said quite enough. Now it's my turn."

"Yes, sir."

"As you know from our previous . . . discussions, Miss Cartwright, I am a devout Methodist, and as such my personal opinion coincides with yours concerning the evil that strong drink does to families. However, of the two books that rule my life, the Holy Bible and this book of Federal Statutes"—he rested his hand on a very thick, leather-bound book on his desk—"in my legal pronouncements, I must rely on the federal statutes as written by the Congress of the United States."

As Margaret started to protest, he again held up his hand. "As I've said before, when you protested my sentencing men to hang, it is not me making the sentence, it is federal law." He shook his head, a rather melancholy expression on his face. "Are you familiar with the term 'black-ink law,' Miss Cartwright?"

When Margaret shook her head, he continued. "Even in the Federal Statutes, there is sometimes ambiguity, and terms such as 'with malice' or 'premeditated' are used, giving the judge, or the jury as the case may be, some discretion in sentencing. However, with black-ink law, there is no gray area, no 'wiggle room' as the lawyers are fond of saying. As is the case here, Miss Cartwright, I have very little choice in the sentence, since no one was harmed by the men's behavior. Drunk and disorderly, with little or no damage to personal property, carries a sentence of no more than thirty days. I cannot change the law, nor, in this case, would I wish to. These men, according to information provided to me by Marshal Madsen in his brief, are apparently law-abiding citizens when not under the influence of whiskey. Therefore, I have no wish to further damage either their reputations or their families' well-being by incarcerating them any longer than I have."

"But, Your Honor—" she started, until he stood up.

"That is all, Miss Cartwright. Court is recessed for one hour," he said, picking up his gavel and banging it on the desk before stalking off toward his chambers.

Margaret whirled on her heels about to leave when she found herself face to face with the handsome man she'd met earlier in the day.

He was tall, slightly over six feet, with narrow hips and broad shoulders. His coal-black hair set off the deep blue of his eyes in a way that made her stomach feel funny and a small shiver start at the back of her neck to run down her spine. He was dressed in a black suit and vest over a starched white shirt, with a small bow tie at his neck. The clothes were of excellent quality and had obviously been tailored by an expert, for they fit his frame like a glove. His knee-high boots were so polished she could see her reflection in them when she let her eyes fall, as proper ladies did when approached by gentlemen in public.

He tipped his hat and inclined his head in a slight bow. "Good afternoon, Miss Cartwright," he said, smiling in a way that caused her to smile back.

"Good afternoon, sir," she replied, unable to remember if he'd introduced himself that morning.

"I am Alexandre Leo LeMat," he said, "and this is Jacques LeDieux, my friend and companion."

She gave a small curtsy. "Pleased to meet you . . . again," she said, trying her best to get the stupid grin off her face, unable to take her gaze from his eyes.

"We would like to invite you to tea, if there is a place to get such in this town."

She debated with herself for a moment. Ladies of breeding were simply not supposed to go out with gentlemen they had not been properly introduced to. It just was not done. However, this was the nineteenth century, was it not? she thought. Perhaps it was time to do away with the conventions of grandmothers and celebrate the new age. Besides, this was the most interesting man she'd met in all her time out West. He even seemed to have a full set of teeth, unlike most of the men she'd seen so far in Fort Smith, and, to make matters even better, it also seemed he bathed regularly . . . also something of a novelty among the men out West.

"I'd be delighted, sir. I do believe the Palace Hotel dining room has a high tea starting at four o'clock."

The man called Leo glanced at a pocket watch.

"Excellent. Then we just have time to make it." He held out his arm, which she took in her right hand. As they walked down the aisle, the little man called Jacques rushed ahead to open the door for them. Margaret thought she detected just the hint of a grin and a glint in the Frenchman's eyes, but she couldn't be certain.

The waiter at the Palace gave Jacques a searching look, his nose turning up ever so slightly at the clothes Jacques was wearing. His attitude changed abruptly when he glanced down at the bill Leo handed him, and he showed them to a corner table near a window looking out on Main Street.

"We'll have tea please," Margaret said, adjusting her skirts so they would not get mussed by her sitting in them.

"Would the gentlemen care for a libation?" the waiter asked.

Margaret glared at him, but softened her glance when Leo said, "No, thank you. We'll just have the tea, also."

She noticed the man introduced as Jacques give a quick scowl, but ignored it, for her attention was fully on Leo.

After the waiter left, Leo asked, "Are you a member of the Temperance movement, Miss Cartwright?"

Margaret nodded. "Yes. As a matter of fact, I

founded the local chapter of the W.C.T.U. here in Fort Smith myself only six months ago."

"W.C.T.U.?" Leo asked.

"Women's Christian Temperance Union," Margaret replied. "I was drawn to it some time ago after hearing a stirring speech by a young woman named Carrie Nation."

"I noticed Judge Parker mentioned something about you also being against executions?" Jacques asked.

"Yes," Margaret answered. "I think capital punishment is nothing less than murder, even if it is sanctioned by the government." She was getting warmed to her subject and could feel her face flush with excitement as it always did when she spoke out against injustice. "And I do not for a minute believe public executions cause other people not to commit crime. Why, just look at the spectacle they make of them, with men selling everything from lemonade to small dolls hanging from miniature scaffolds."

"I did not know the purpose of the hangings was to prevent *other* people from killing," Jacques observed wryly. "I thought it was to punish those who did and to keep *them* from killing again." He grinned. "And, to give the government credit, I do not know of a single case where a hanged man has ever committed another crime."

"But, Mr. LeDieux, can't you see how executing

men for killing someone makes the government no better than they are?"

Jacques was saved from making a reply by the arrival of their waiter with tea. It was served in a silver pot, with cream and sugar and lemon slices arranged neatly on the tray. There were three small plates covered with pastry.

"Here are your tea and biscuits, madame," the waiter said, placing the tray on the table before them and leaving Margaret to do the serving.

"Biscuits?" Jacques said, picking up one of the small pastries. "These look like cookies to me."

"Biscuit is the English term for cookies, *mon ami*," Leo said. "I believe they call our biscuits crumpets."

Jacques shook his head. "And I thought Cajuns made a mess of the English language. It seems the English are even worse."

Margaret laughed, beginning to like the small Frenchman more and more. Though he looked as rough as a cob on the exterior, she could tell by his soft-spoken way he was as gentle as a lamb on the inside.

"You are right, Mr. LeDieux," Margaret said, handing him a cup of tea. "I've heard it said Americans and English are very similar people separated by a common language."

"*Oui*, mademoiselle," Jacques said, taking the tea from her hand. "Like the French and the Creole, both speak the same tongue, but in very different ways."

Now even Leo laughed, making Margaret smile. *He has a very nice laugh,* she thought. It made a woman want to do something funny and gay just to hear it.

After Leo took a sip of his tea and a bite of a biscuit, he looked into Margaret's eyes. "I am very interested in your thoughts on capital punishment, Miss Cartwright," he said. "How would you deal with some of these men to whom other people's lives have no meaning?"

"Why," she said, more than a little surprised that such a distinguished man would ask her opinion on what was generally considered a man's topic of discussion, "if the prisoner expressed no remorse for his killings, then I would simply lock him away so he could do no further harm."

"But, mademoiselle," Jacques said, leaning forward and trying to balance his tea cup on his thigh, "if the killer escaped and managed to kill again, would you not feel some guilt at the loss of innocent life due to your leniency?"

She raised her eyebrows and stared at Jacques for a moment, not sure if she was being teased or not. "Of course not," she said, shortly. "If that were to happen, the death would be on the prison officials who allowed the man to escape, not on those who showed him compassion."

"I'm sure that would be a great solace to the person who was killed," Jacques murmured as he lowered his head and took a sip of his tea, wrinkling his nose at the taste.

Leo, to change the subject, asked Margaret about the cultural activities in Fort Smith, specifically about whether there was any opera or theater to be attended.

After an enjoyable afternoon of tea and conversation, they parted, with Leo holding Margaret's hand a few seconds longer than necessary as he said good-bye, making her heart flutter.

"Perhaps," she said, looking down and blushing at her forwardness, "we may do this again sometime."

Leo's eyes bored into hers. "No, I would much rather take you to dinner tomorrow night, if it would please you," he said.

"Oh, I couldn't . . . it wouldn't be proper for me to go out with a man alone," she replied, not believing she was turning his offer down.

He frowned for a moment, then suggested, "Perhaps you have a lady friend who could accompany us? Would that make it proper?"

Margaret thought for a moment, then nodded rapidly. "Yes, as a matter of fact, I do." She looked at Jacques. "She is very pretty, and I do think you two would enjoy each other's company very much."

"But, Mademoiselle Cartwright . . ." Jacques began, a look of stark terror in his eyes.

"He would be happy to join us, wouldn't you, Jacques?" Leo interrupted firmly.

Jacques glanced at Leo, then nodded, his lips tight and a slight flush on his face.

Margaret reached into her purse and withdrew a small card. "Here is my address. You may call at seven tomorrow. Gretchen and I will be waiting."

# Chapter 7

After Margaret walked away, Leo and Jacques stood for a moment on the front steps of the Palace Hotel. Leo took a deep breath, looking around at the bustling activity of Fort Smith.

It wasn't all that bad a town, he thought, especially in the fall, after the searing heat of the Arkansas summer had passed.

"Come, my friend," he said to Jacques, "let's go see if Judge Parker has time to grant us an interview."

He glanced at Jacques and noticed his companion had a sullen, dark expression on his face. It wasn't like his friend to be so surly for no reason.

"What's the matter, Jacques? Why the long face?" he asked, concern in his voice.

Jacques glared at him for a moment without speaking.

"Have I done something to make you angry?" Leo asked.

"Oh, no," Jacques replied. "Nothing of any consequence. You have just arranged, without my permission, for me to go out for the evening with a woman named Gretchen." He stopped and looked seriously at Leo, his nose wrinkled as if he'd smelled something sour in a sauce he was preparing for supper. "Leo, have you ever met anyone named Gretchen who was even marginally attractive?" he asked.

Leo started to answer and was interrupted by his Cajun friend. "No, of course you haven't," Jacques went on. "In all probability, she will outweigh the two of us combined and will have a moustache to rival that of Wyatt Earp . . . that is unless she shaves on a daily basis, which also is probable in this godforsaken town."

Leo laughed. "Why, Jacques, look on the bright side. She might be most comely."

"No, *mon ami*, Margaret is pretty, and it is a well-known fact that only ugly women hang around with pretty ones. The chance of two female friends both being fair is about the same as finding a chef in this town that does not overcook the meat in a meal."

"You worry too much, Jacques," Leo said in his most reasonable tone. "Why not wait until tomorrow night and see what this Gretchen is actually like before you complain about her?"

Jacques shook his head. "I do not know, Leo. I

have this terrible feeling in the pit of my stomach that tomorrow is going to be a disaster rivaled only by the sale of the Louisiana Territory to the United States."

"That feeling you have is probably from the tea you drank," Leo observed, a faint smile on his lips. "Obviously, your stomach is unused to having a non-alcoholic beverage in it. Perhaps a beer or two would make it feel better?"

Jacques's expression brightened marginally. "Well, it certainly would not hurt, would it?" He stroked the scar on his cheek contemplatively. "After all, beer is second only to wine as a restorative of good humor."

"Come on, then. We can stop by one of the saloons that line the streets and have a drink. We need to give the judge time to finish his afternoon session in any case before we ask him for an appointment."

Prisoner Mike Blake grabbed his stomach, bent over, and gave out with a loud moan. The evening guard at the Hell on the Border Jail underneath the Fort Smith courthouse, John Whitmire, ambled over to look through the cell bars at the stricken man as he writhed on the floor.

"Hey, Mike," he drawled, apparently unconcerned with Blake's evident pain. "What happened? You eat too much of that slop we call supper?"

"Oh, John, I think I'm dyin," Blake said, moaning again and rolling around on the floor.

"Shit!" Whitmire muttered. He looked around until he saw another guard over by the jail door. "Hey, Sonny. Open the door for a minute. We got another one for the infirmary."

Sonny took a row of keys off his belt and unlocked the jail door, stepping back with his hand on the butt of a pistol in his holster in case any of the other hundred and fifty men in the small, dungeonlike room tried to make a break for it.

Whitmire put his hands under Blake's shoulders and helped him to his feet, then led him through the door and up three flights of stairs to the room on the top floor of the building that served as makeshift infirmary for the jail.

Whitmire unlocked the door and helped Blake inside the room and over to one of the beds that lined the wall.

Ed Rhodes, a prisoner who'd volunteered to act as nurse for the sick and injured men in the infirmary, approached the bed and stared down at Blake. "What's the matter with Mike?" he asked Whitmire.

The guard grinned. "He ate too much, I suppose. Got the bellyache." He shook his head and scratched his chin. "You fellers oughta know better'n to eat too much of that crap at one time."

Ed glanced over his shoulder at the other inmate nurse. "Well, seems we're gettin' a full house here. I guess Isaac and I will take another shift to help out," he said, pointing at the other nurse, Isaac Martin, who looked up and nodded at Whitmire.

"All right. No skin off my nose," the guard said and started toward the door.

"Hey, Johnny," Rhodes said.

The man stopped and looked back. "Yeah?"

"Tell the cook to try and get some meat that ain't two weeks old 'fore he cooks it, all right?"

Whitmire grinned. "I'll be sure an' tell him how to run his kitchen . . . when hell freezes over."

After the guard left, Martin and Rhodes gathered next to the bed Blake was lying on. "So, you got my message?" Rhodes asked.

"Yeah, but why in hell did you want me to pretend to be sick?" Blake asked, sitting up in bed, the mask of pain gone completely from his face.

"Isaac an' me, we found a bar that's been half cut in two up here. Somebody must've done it with a saw an' then put mud on the cuts so they wouldn't be noticed. We're gonna make a run for it tonight."

Blake looked dubious. "Hell, man, we're three

stories up. Even if we get out the window, what're we gonna do then? Fly away?"

Isaac Martin smiled and bent down to reach under the bed. He pulled out a long rope made of many blankets tied together. "No, we ain't gonna fly. We're gonna climb down this to the ground."

Blake winced. "You sure that'll hold us?"

Rhodes shrugged. "So what if it don't? Dyin' quick in a fall is better'n staying in the Hell on the Border, ain't it?"

"Dyin' yes, gettin' all broken up inside an' still bein' in here ain't so appetizin'," Blake replied.

Rhodes grabbed him by the shirt. "Quit your whinin'. You in or out?"

Blake pushed his hands away. "In," he said, before adding, "Though I'm damned if I know why."

"Good," Rhodes said. "Then get your sorry butt over here and help us bend these bars back."

It was almost seven in the evening before Judge Parker finished his day in court. Leo was astonished to learn that the man worked almost twelve hours a day hearing cases. It was a load that would kill most men, or cause them to take their work much less seriously than Judge Parker evidently did.

Parker's bailiff reluctantly showed them into his chambers, warning them not to stay too long. "The judge has had a very hard day. Please do not keep him from his supper any longer than is necessary," he asked.

"I assure you," Leo said, "our business will only take a few minutes of his time."

When they entered, Leo was struck by Parker's appearance. He was seated at his desk, reading briefs of the cases he'd presided over that day. His face was pale and drawn, and he looked as if he'd lost several pounds during the course of the day. The man was working himself to death, Leo thought, staring at him with a physician's trained eye.

Parker looked up and waved them toward his desk. "Come in, gentlemen," he said in a voice lower and less forceful than the one he'd used in the courtroom.

"Good evening, Judge Parker," Leo said as he and Jacques took seats before his desk.

"What can I do for you?" Parker asked, his voice tired and without energy.

"My name is Doctor Leo LeMat," Leo said, "and this is my friend Jacques LeDieux." He reached over and handed the judge one of his cards.

Parker put the glasses he had on a ribbon around his neck onto his nose and peered at the card. "Leo LeMat, Portraitist, Gun for Hire," he read out loud.

His eyes narrowed slightly as he returned his gaze to Leo. "A strange combination, Mr. LeMat," he said. "And just which of these two professions causes you to come to see me? Are you looking to hire on as one of my marshals?"

Leo wagged his head. "No, Judge Parker. For the past several years I've been painting portraits of famous, and infamous, Western characters. The last two were Bill Hickok and Wyatt Earp. I traveled to Fort Smith from San Antonio, Texas, to see if you would be so kind as to sit for one of my paintings."

Parker sat back in his chair, still holding Leo's card, staring at Leo. A slight smile appeared on his tired face. "And which category do I fit in, Mr. LeMat? Famous . . . or infamous?"

Leo returned the smile, relieved at the judge's initial reaction to his request. "Famous, sir, of course."

Parker glanced around at his desk, covered with briefs and law books and other correspondence. He spread his hands over the mess. "Well, Dr. LeMat, as you can see, I am very busy with the court's business just now. From the little I know of portrait painting, it requires long hours sitting while the painter does his work. I just don't know that I could spare the time."

Leo thought for a moment. "Perhaps I could make it easier on you, Judge Parker. If I might be allowed to sit in the back of the courtroom while you heard cases, I could make my preliminary sketches while you worked. I would then only need a couple of days of formal sitting, and we might do those on the weekends."

Parker held up his hand. "Perhaps it could be arranged. However, I could not sit for you on the Sabbath. My Sundays are reserved for church worship and family time."

Leo nodded. "I understand. Then you would have no objection to my drawing you in the courtroom?"

Parker was about to answer when the bailiff burst into the room, shouting, "Judge Parker, there's been a jailbreak!"

Parker quickly rose to his feet. "What's happened, John?"

"Ed Rhodes and Isaac Martin were detailed as nurses in the old jail. Evidently, they loosened one of the bars on the window during their early shift. This evening, they volunteered to spend another night with the sick. Just a while ago, they forced the bar and escaped with one of the patients, a man named Mike Blake."

"Are they armed?" Parker asked.

"Yes, sir. They broke into the armory and stole some rifles and pistols before they left the building."

"Where were the guards?"

"Uh . . . evidently they were having their supper and were away from their posts for a short while."

Parker nodded, an angry expression on his face. "Well, we'll deal with them later. Are there any marshals available to track the men?"

The bailiff shrugged. "The only one in town right now is Chris Madsen. Heck Thomas and Bill Tilghman are on their way in with some prisoners, but they won't arrive until tomorrow or the next day."

Parker stroked his chin, thinking for a moment, then he glanced down at Leo's card lying on his desk. "Dr. LeMat, is your card correct? Do you hire out your gun?"

"Well, Your Honor . . ." Leo began.

"You asked me for a favor, Dr. LeMat; now I'm asking you for one. These men that escaped are vicious murderers and rapists. They need to be apprehended as soon as possible, and it's a job for more than one man. If you let me hire you for one or two days, until they are caught, then I will agree to sit for your painting. Is it a deal?"

Leo glanced at Jacques. "If I can use my friend Jacques to help, then it's a deal."

"Raise your right hands and repeat after me."

After he swore Leo and Jacques in as deputy U.S. marshals, Parker opened his desk drawer and flipped them a couple of badges. "The pay is normally a dollar and a half a day, plus reimbursement for expenses and miles traveled, but since you're only going to be on the payroll for one or two days, I'll make it five dollars a day. Is that all right?"

Leo nodded, thinking it was less than a tenth of his usual fee, but if it convinced the judge to sit for him, it would be worth it.

They pinned on the badges and departed the judge's chambers quickly, going to the hotel to get Jacques's shotgun and some more ammunition for Leo's pistol.

"Leo, what the judge is paying us will not even cover the cost of our supper tomorrow night. We should have asked for more money," Jacques complained.

Leo shook his head. "No, my friend. By doing this favor for Judge Parker, it will ensure his cooperation for my portrait of him. I would have done it for free if he'd asked."

As Jacques broke open Ange, his pet name for his shotgun, and put shells in the barrels and his pockets, he began to mutter to himself in French.

"What did you say?" Leo asked.

"I said, first you commit me to have dinner with a woman who will undoubtedly turn out to be the approximate size and shape of a beef cow, and then you sell my services for slave wages." He shook his head. "I knew I should have stayed in San Antonio."

"But think of all the fun you'd have missed," Leo said, breaking open the loading gate on his Baby LeMat pistol and checking his loads. "Running through the night, chasing desperados who are murderers and rapists and perhaps getting shot at." He snapped the gate shut and put the pistol in his shoulder holster.

"What an adventure!" Leo said, his eyes lighting up and his face flushing with excitement.

"Yes, what fun," Jacques said dryly. "Perhaps tomorrow we can stand in front of a stampede of angry cattle or get involved in a bar fight to add to our 'adventure.' "

Leo shook his head, grinning at his friend. "One would almost think you'd rather be back home, sitting on the veranda of our hotel, bored and complaining that there is nothing exciting to do in San Antonio after dark," Leo said.

"At least no one would be shooting at us in San Antonio," Jacques said, snapping the double barrels of Ange shut.

Leo headed out the door. "You worry too much, my friend," he called over his shoulder.

"With you," Jacques muttered as he followed Leo, "one cannot worry enough!"

# Chapter 8

Isaac Martin, Ed Rhodes, and Mike Blake ran as fast as they could through the night toward a copse of woods across the field from the Hell on the Border Jail. The night was hot and humid and they were covered with sweat, their prison clothes sticking to them like damp rags.

They were hampered somewhat in their attempt to escape by Blake, who was limping badly on his right leg. Just as he'd feared, the makeshift rope of blankets had given way while he was still fifteen feet from the ground. He landed badly on his right ankle, turning it under with an audible pop as the tendons snapped. Within minutes, the ankle had swollen to almost twice its size, bulging over his work shoes with the skin turning a dark, angry-looking blue color.

"Come on, Blake," Rhodes whispered savagely, "hurry up. They're gonna be on our back trail in a few minutes."

"I'm comin' fast as I can, damn it! I think I broke my fuckin' leg," Blake replied, grimacing in pain as he hobbled after the other two men over uneven ground.

They had to pass the hangman's scaffold to get to the woods, and all three men superstitiously avoided looking at the stark white structure that loomed overhead.

Blake, who'd been a Catholic early in his life, though never seriously enough to keep him from raping a schoolteacher one sunny afternoon, crossed himself and whispered a quick prayer for help from the Virgin Mother. It was the first time he'd prayed in fifteen years, but the words came to him as if from some dark cavern of his mind.

After making it to cover of the forest, Martin and Rhodes stopped to check the loads in the Winchesters they'd stolen from the jail's armory.

Blake had grabbed a short-barreled American Arms shotgun but hadn't been smart enough to take extra shells, so he was limited to two shots.

Martin looked up, satisfied his rifle had its full complement of seven shells in the magazine. "Another coupla hundred yards an' we'll be through the woods. This trail comes out over near the road outta town an' maybe we'll get lucky and catch a passerby with a wagon or some horses."

Blake shook his head sorrowfully. "If we do,

it'll be the first time I ever got lucky in my whole miserable life."

"Hell, boy," Rhodes said, slapping him on the shoulder, "you was lucky when you met us, wasn't ya?"

Blake glanced down at his ankle, which was swelling even more and was throbbing like it was on fire, and he wondered if it had indeed been good luck or bad when he befriended the men who'd gotten him into this mess.

He glanced up at the moon, shaking his head. There was little chance anyone would be out and about in a wagon at this time of night, and he knew he couldn't walk on his foot much farther. He was going back to that stinkhole, there wasn't any doubt in his mind.

Leo and Jacques returned from their hotel room fully armed just in time to hear Marshal Chris Madsen talking with Judge Isaac Parker.

"Damn it, Judge," the marshal was saying. "It's only three men I'm goin' after. I don't need any help, 'specially from some pilgrims from outta town."

"This isn't one of your frontier cow towns, Chris," Parker replied, looking over his shoulder at Leo and Jacques standing nearby. "This is Fort Smith, home of the federal district court. I don't want these men on the streets any longer than is necessary, and God help us all if they kill some innocent citizens after escaping from our jail. We'd never hear the end of it."

Madsen choked back an angry reply about the incompetence of jailers who'd let three men walk right out of the jail and merely nodded.

After Judge Parker introduced him to Leo and Jacques, Madsen said, "Come on, LeMat. We'll start over at the jail," and started off at a rapid pace without waiting to see if Leo and Jacques were following.

The three men stood next to the jail wall, with its blanket rope still hanging from the third-story window.

Madsen bent over to examine the boot prints in the soft dirt next to the wall, then he straightened, pointing. "Looks like they went that way, toward those woods over yonder."

Leo glanced at the tracks, a thoughtful expression on his face. "Evidently one of the men was injured in the escape."

"What do you mean?" Madsen asked, glancing at Leo with upraised eyebrows, wondering how the devil he knew that.

Leo pointed. "See how the tracks of one of them are not symmetrical? He's taking longer strides with his left foot than he is with his right." Leo pointed to where the rope was frayed and broken ten feet from the ground, with a shorter piece of the blankets lying on the dirt next to the wall. "I'd say he hurt his right leg in the climb down the rope when it broke, causing him to fall the last ten feet."

"How'd you figure that out?"

"My friend is a medical doctor," Jacques explained as his eyes searched the darkness nearby.

"Great! Just what I need to help me catch three murderers. A sawbones," Madsen said.

"I assure you we will not let you down, Marshal," Leo said, a slight smile curling his lips.

"You'd better not!" Madsen growled and pulled his pistol from its holster as he started toward the forest across the field.

The moonlight, though faint, was enough to let them see the tracks of the escapees well enough to follow them through the tangle of undergrowth and bushes in the forest, until they came out on the other side near a wide road.

Two hundred yards down the road, they could see dark shadows next to a large buckboard that was stopped.

"That looks like it might be our culprits," Leo said in a low whisper, inclining his head toward the wagon.

"LeMat, you and Jacques cross on over the road and head up on the other side. I'll go this way and maybe we can get 'em between us in a cross fire," Madsen said, crouching and moving slowly away.

Leo nodded and he and Jacques took off in a lope across the road and toward the buckboard in the distance, watching as they ran to make sure the men there didn't catch sight of them as they moved alongside the road.

When they got closer, Leo could see three men talking with another, who had his hands raised in the air. "They're stealing that man's wagon," he whispered to Jacques.

Jacques eased back the hammers on Ange. His teeth gleamed in the moonlight as he grinned. "It will be the last thing they ever steal, if my Ange has anything to say about it," he growled in a low, harsh voice.

The prospect of gunplay always made Jacques happy, for he was at heart a man of action who got quickly bored if too many days went by without something happening to get his blood flowing.

Madsen stood up and aimed his pistol at the men with an outstretched arm as he shouted, "Put your weapons down and hold up your hands!"

He was answered by the explosion from Blake's shotgun, twin fat fingers of flame leaping from the barrels as the murderer fired at the marshal from the hip.

Madsen yelled, spinning around as two of the

buckshot pellets took him in the left arm. The force of the slugs knocked him to the ground.

Leo jerked his Baby LeMat from his shoulder holster just as Jacques rose to his feet and fired Ange, aiming low.

Blake's feet were knocked out from under him as molten slugs tore into his legs, shredding his calves down to the bone and shattering his legs.

As he screamed, Martin and Rhodes both began to fire their Winchesters at the two figures standing in dark shadows next to the road.

Leo ducked instinctively as bullets whined by overhead and he snapped off two quick shots, firing by instinct without taking time to aim properly.

The first one hit Isaac Martin in the middle of his stomach, smacking into a silver belt buckle, doubling him over as if he'd been gut-punched by a heavyweight boxer.

Leo's second shot missed Rhodes, but was close enough to drive him behind the wagon, where he leaned his rifle on the side of the buckboard and continued to fire despite the plunging of the harness horse.

Jacques punched two more shells into his express gun and snapped it shut, just as Leo fired the shotgun cylinder on his LeMat pistol. The grapeshot tore into the side of the wagon where Rhodes was hiding, shredding wood into hundreds of splinters that ricocheted into his face and eyes. He screamed and dropped his rifle, coming out from behind the wagon with his hands covering his ruined face, shouting, "Don't shoot . . . don't shoot . . . I give up!"

When Leo and Jacques approached, they found Rhodes with a number of splinters sticking out of his face, making him look like a strange breed of porcupine, while Martin was doubled over holding his stomach and moaning in pain. Blake was unconscious, blood spurting from his torn, ragged legs.

Leo holstered his pistol and grabbed a bandanna from Blake's neck. "Jacques, go see if Marshal Madsen is all right while I try to stop this bleeding," he said, wrapping the bandanna tightly above the wound that was pumping blood.

"God damn!" Blake cried in pain. "You're killin' me!"

"Lie still," Leo said in a firm voice, "or you will surely die from loss of blood."

Two hours later, Judge Parker met with Marshal Madsen, Leo, and Jacques in his chambers. He opened his right-hand desk drawer and took out a bottle of brandy. Placing three glasses on the desk, he poured healthy measures into each.

"Aren't you going to join us?" Leo asked as he took up his glass.

Parker shook his head. "No. As a general rule,

I disapprove of strong spirits. But I'm realistic enough to know that when men have faced death in battle, they sometimes require more than a pat on the back. Good work, gentlemen," he said, nodding his head toward the glasses.

The marshal, his left arm in a sling and with a bandage on it that Leo had applied, raised his glass in a toast. "I hate to admit it, men, but I was wrong. Thanks for the help out there, Leo. You, too, Jacques."

After they drank, Madsen looked at the judge. "Judge, I don't think I've ever seen such good shootin' as these two men displayed tonight. We managed to apprehend all three escapees without anybody gettin' killed, though I hear Blake may lose one of his legs."

Leo shook his head. "I don't think so, Marshal. I spoke with the prison doctor and advised him of some new techniques I've read about to keep suppuration at bay. It involves washing the wound with carbolic acid on a daily basis. If all goes well, Mr. Blake should recover with nothing worse than a slight limp."

"Gentlemen," Judge Parker said, refilling their glasses, "as I said, you have my thanks, and," he added to Leo, "I have a debt to pay concerning a portrait, I believe."

"I shall begin tomorrow, if that's all right, Judge."

Parker glanced at Madsen. "Dr. LeMat is going to make me famous, Chris, by painting my portrait."

Madsen glanced out the judge's window at the scaffold standing guard over the field below, thinking that platform had already made the judge famous.

# Chapter 9

Leo couldn't get his mind off Margaret Cartwright. Her beauty, her easy laugh, and even the intensity of her belief in herself and her cause were very intriguing to him.

Leo couldn't get his mind off Margaret Cartwright. Her beauty, her easy laugh, and even the intensity of her belief in herself and her cause were very intriguing to him.

In the years since his wife had died in childbirth, he'd been out with a number of women. Some he'd dated because of their intellect, their appreciation of fine music, cuisine, or simply because they were easy to talk to and exchange ideas with. Others had attracted him due to their extreme beauty and grace. This was the first time in his memory he'd found a woman with both an excellent mind, committed to ideals she felt would make the world a better place to live in, and beauty equal to or surpassing any of his previous woman friends.

Even the prospect of Judge Parker agreeing to sit for his portrait failed to take his mind off Margaret and the effect she was having on him.

He was looking forward to their dinner this evening, and he hoped Jacques wouldn't spoil it if his guest were, as his friend put it, of the approximate size and shape of a beef cow.

Leo sat in the rear of the Fort Smith federal courtroom, his sketching pad perched on his knees, a long stick of charcoal in his right hand, trying to get the picture of Margaret out of his thoughts so he could concentrate on the job at hand, capturing a likeness of Judge Isaac Parker on paper. He had to squint slightly to make out the nuances of Judge Parker's visage due to the poor lighting of the place, but the judge had a very strong face, one full of character and strength and, contrary to what many of his detractors in the press wrote, compassion for the men who came before him to be sentenced.

With a few deft strokes he outlined the face and head, trying to do nothing more at the present than get the general look right. He knew to get the steely determination in Parker's eyes correct, he'd have to make a much closer and more detailed inspection with the judge in better light.

As he sketched, Leo listened with half an ear to the pleadings in the cases brought before the judge. He found, much to his surprise, after all he'd read about how quick the judge was to sentence men to be hanged, that Parker listened to all the evidence presented, even prompting the defense attorneys in some instances when they seemed to be letting the prosecution get away with too many assumptions concerning the guilt of the defendants.

The judge, to his credit, was managing to ignore Leo's presence in his court, focusing his entire attention on the cases before him this morning. Leo could see why the work of the court was so tiring for the judge, since he seemed to concentrate to a degree that almost seemed impossible considering the long hours of the court.

The man sitting in the defendant's chair this morning was accused of murder. The prosecutor said his name was Cherokee Bill, otherwise known as Crawford Goldsby.

Leo stopped his drawing when the man's name was announced. In his constant research about men of the West, Leo had read about this particular desperado many times over the past couple of years. Cherokee Bill was part Cherokee, part white, part Mexican, and part Negro. While just a teenager, he'd fallen in with two young criminals, Bill and Jim Cook, and he'd killed a lawman when a posse tried to arrest one of the Cook brothers.

After this, Cherokee Bill teamed up with the Cook gang and over the next few years committed a series of notorious killings and robberies that made all the San Antonio newspapers. He gunned down his brother-in-law for beating his sister; while looting a depot he murdered station agent Richard Richards; and he'd killed conductor Samuel Collins when Collins tried to throw him off a train for not having a ticket. He'd been visiting his sweetheart in Lenapah, Oklahoma, when he was captured and brought before Judge Parker.

In spite of his efforts to ignore the proceedings, Leo watched fascinated as Parker asked the man to stand before him after all the testimony was in.

Parker pursed his lips, staring down at Cherokee Bill over the rims of his half-glasses. "Crawford Goldsby, alias Cherokee Bill, you have shown remarkable disrespect for not only the laws of this territory, but for the lives of your fellow man your entire life. You leave me no choice but to sentence you to hang by the neck until you are dead."

Leo watched Goldsby's face as the sentence was handed down. Goldsby's eyes were the flat black of the rattlesnake, cold and deep and without any of the light of human compassion in them. The still-young man showed no emotion whatsoever when the judge told him he was to be hanged, leading Leo to wonder if there was something missing in Goldsby's makeup that made him incapable of worrying about his death, as he'd seemed incapable of being concerned with the deaths of the many other men he'd killed.

Goldsby's mother and sister, sitting in the front row of the courtroom, gasped and sobbed, holding each other as the verdict was handed down.

Leo noticed Parker's gaze flick to the family of the condemned man, and he thought for a moment he could see tears well up in the judge's eyes. Leo thought the judge probably felt he was sentencing the family to a kind of death as well as the defendant. It was amazing, Leo mused, how rarely desperados considered the effects that their crimes had on the ones who loved them.

Cherokee Bill turned to his mother and sister and for the first time a flicker of emotion crossed his face. He gave a grim smile. "Don't worry none, Ma. They ain't hanged me yet," he said in a soft voice that didn't match the rough look of his face and clothes.

As the bailiffs led Cherokee Bill away, manacles on his wrists and ankles, Parker abruptly banged his gavel, a look of sadness on his face. "Court is recessed for thirty minutes."

Leo checked his pocket watch and noticed it was almost the noon hour. He had better go to the hotel and see if Jacques was ready for lunch, he thought, putting his sketchpad and charcoal away in a valise.

As Leo walked toward the rear door of the courtroom, he noticed Marshal Chris Madsen talking with two other men in the adjoining hallway.

He nodded and prepared to pass them by, but Madsen stopped him.

"Doctor LeMat," the lawman said, "I'd like you to meet a couple of friends of mine."

Leo stopped and looked at the two men.

"This is Marshal Bill Tilghman and Marshal Heck Thomas," Madsen said.

Leo stuck out his hand. "I'm very pleased to meet you both. I've heard a great deal about your exploits over the last few years."

As the two men shook Leo's hand, Madsen said, "Dr. LeMat is the man I told you about who helped me bring in the escapees the other day. He's quite handy with a short-gun."

Leo noticed the badge Tilghman wore was hammered out of what looked to be two twenty-dollar gold pieces. He was well over six feet tall, lean, with a rounded, pleasant face and a large, bushy handlebar moustache. His hair was light brown and his eyes hazel. All in all, Leo thought, a striking-looking man who would make a fine subject for a portrait.

Thomas, who appeared to Leo to be somewhat older than Tilghman, was of a heavier build, with dark hair and moustache and a square jaw. Everything about the man radiated seriousness of purpose and Leo wondered if he had any sense of humor at all and if he took himself as seriously as he seemed to.

"I hear you're in town to paint the judge's picture," Tilghman said, a slight grin on his face.

Thomas gave a short cough. "I never heard of a painter who was good with a gun before." He hesitated, then added, "Nor a doctor, neither."

Madsen grunted. "Oh, what about Doc Holliday?"

"Doc's a dentist, that don't count," Thomas replied.

"To answer your question, Marshal Tilghman, I did come to Fort Smith with the idea of painting Judge Parker's portrait. Capturing famous men of the West on canvas is a . . . hobby of mine." He looked from one to the other of the three men standing before him. "As a matter of fact, I'd be honored if you all would agree to sit for me also."

Thomas shook his head almost before the words were out of Leo's mouth. "I ain't got time for such foolishness. I just came to get some supplies and get back on the trail of Bill Doolin."

Tilghman looked at Madsen. "Whatta you say, Chris? I think it might be kinda fun."

Madsen glanced at Thomas. "Only if Heck agrees. That is, if he can get the Doolin Gang off his mind long enough."

Tilghman looked at Leo and explained, "Heck has a thing about the Doolins. He's been on their trail for some time now an' he's afraid somebody else is gonna get 'em 'fore he does."

"I told you I don't have the time," Thomas said. "I heard the Doolin Gang just robbed a train over near Dover, Oklahoma. Red Buck killed a preacher in the getaway, an' I'm damned if I'm gonna let 'em get away this time."

"I guess we'll have to pass, LeMat," Tilghman said, a note of regret in his voice.

Leo nodded. "Well, perhaps the opportunity will present itself before I leave town. Good day, gentlemen," he said, tipping his hat. As he left, he thought Tilghman was indeed the showman his press clippings claimed him to be. It was evident from the way the man dressed he didn't exactly shy away from attention.

Leo walked to the Star Hotel, finding Jacques sitting on the porch, smoking a cigar and watching the women pass by on the boardwalk while he drank a glass of red wine.

"Hello, Jacques," Leo said, putting his valise on an empty chair and sitting next to his friend.

Jacques gave him a look, his eyes flat. "Hello, Leo."

"I see you are in no better mood this afternoon than you were last evening."

Jacques took a deep drag off the cigar and tilted smoke from his nostrils. "I have been passing the time observing various womenfolk as they pass the hotel," he said. "I am looking for one so ugly that horses shy when she approaches. One that dogs follow thinking she is some strange breed of animal that might be kin."

Leo shook his head, trying to suppress a chuckle at his friend's surly attitude. "Are you still convinced that this Gretchen you are to have dinner with tonight is going to be so bad?"

Jacques looked at him. "Is there any doubt, *mon ami* ?"

"Of course there is," Leo replied. "Margaret said the woman is quite fair."

"Of course she would say that. She wants to have dinner with you and this is her only chance. I'm surprised she didn't add that all the other women like Gretchen and she makes fine quilts— the standard description of a woman so unattractive she could only get a male by sewing a quilt and throwing it over his head so he couldn't see her face."

Leo laughed out loud. "Jacques, perhaps we should try to find some food for you. I'm afraid your hunger is making you delirious."

"Yes, let us do that, Leo. Maybe I will get lucky and contract food poisoning and not be able to accompany you on your outing tonight."

"You would do that to your friend, when you know how much I'm looking forward to this evening?"

Jacques sighed. "Friendship is a wonderful thing,

Leo. For the sake of ours, I would face down a crowd of men with guns and knives to protect you. I would stand in front of a runaway team of horses to pull you to safety, but even friendship has its limits." He stubbed out his cigar in an ashtray on the table and stood up.

"And, I'm very much afraid being seen in public with a woman such as this Gretchen is bound to be is testing those limits."

As they walked toward a restaurant, Jacques added, "Perhaps I should step off the boardwalk and stroll in the street so that I might get run over by a wagon."

"Not before lunch, Jacques," Leo said. "It is very poor form to be run over on an empty stomach."

Jacques looked sideways at his friend. "That very much depends on the food one has consumed, *mon ami*. Considering the typical cuisine out West, being run over by a wagon is a more than fitting dessert."

Leo shook his head, exasperated. "Jacques, after we eat, I want you to go back to the hotel and take a nap. Perhaps it will make your mood better."

"Take a nap?" Jacques protested. "Like a little child?"

"Yes."

"I haven't taken a nap since I was three," Jacques said huffily.

"Yes, and your disposition shows it," Leo said.

"After you nap, you can treat yourself to a bath and a shave at the barber's."

"Why should I bother to get clean for a date with a cow?"

"Don't do it for her, do it for me," Leo said, "otherwise I will insist we sit at different tables."

Jacques looked horrified. "You'd leave me alone with this creature?" he asked.

"Only if you make me," Leo said.

# Chapter 10

Jacques and Leo headed toward Madame Abigail's Boarding House, the place where Margaret said she and several other young, single women stayed. She'd explained Mrs. Abigail Pringle was like a mother to the girls, endeavoring to keep them out of trouble and with unsullied reputations, a feat not easy in a town as rough and tumble as Fort Smith.

There were strict rules, and to break them meant instant expulsion from the boarding house. The rules, according to Abigail, were merely common sense, such as no one out after dark alone, no gentlemen callers other than in the sitting room, and then only if another girl or two was present, and the girls could never go out with gentlemen alone.

"This place sounds more like one of those exclusive schools such as you have Angeline attending than a boarding house," Jacques commented as they walked.

"You're right, my friend," Leo replied. "Of course, in towns such as Fort Smith, on the border of the wildest of territories, I suppose having such strict rules is necessary for the protection of single women."

Jacques gave a short laugh. "I think you give women too little credit, *mon ami*. The women I've been acquainted with, both here in the West and back home in New Orleans, have always been perfectly capable of taking care of themselves, especially where men were concerned."

Leo glanced at Jacques, trying to keep from smiling. "Yes, but the women you've been acquainted with were . . . how shall I say this . . . of a somewhat different nature than Margaret and her friends."

Jacques stopped, his hands on his hips. "And just what does that remark mean? As I recall, they were the same women you used to go out with and fight over when we were young bucks prowling the streets and back alleys of New Orleans."

Leo finally laughed out loud. "I meant to cast no aspersions, Jacques. It's just that those were . . . women of the world, so to speak, used to taking care of themselves and dealing with men. It's my feeling here that Margaret and her friends are more innocent, more naive, when it comes to members of the opposite sex."

Jacques shook his head, a smile curling the ends

of his lips. "It is you, my friend, who sounds remarkably naive," Jacques said. "Women, whether they reside in New Orleans or in the Oklahoma Territory, are never as innocent as you seem to believe. They are taught at their mothers' knees, probably before they are able to walk, how to deal with men in their later lives."

Leo cut his eyes toward his friend. "And how is that?" he asked.

Jacques shrugged. "It is simplicity itself, Leo. Men, for the most part, want only one thing from the women they pursue . . . the one thing women have that men can get nowhere else: their love. They are taught, I am sure, to withhold this love just out of a man's reach until he is driven crazy with desire. Then, they offer it to him at the most expensive price in the world, a marriage contract."

"You have become most cynical in your old age, Jacques," Leo observed, returning Jacques's smile.

They started walking again. "However," Jacques continued, "I'm quite sure this Gretchen I'm to accompany is in fact quite innocent where men are concerned. I am probably the only one that has ever been foolish enough to take her out in public."

Leo shook his head, giving a quick, silent wish that Jacques was wrong, and that Gretchen would be no worse than plain, or he knew he would never hear the end of it from his friend. He did not look forward to spending the rest of their time in Fort Smith listening to Jacques telling him he told him so.

They arrived at Madame Abigail's, an imposing three-story Victorian house on a side street next to a church.

"That figures," Jacques said, looking at the steeple next door. "This Abigail woman probably has a tunnel connecting the two places so she can have the girls go to church every day, rain or shine."

Leo thought Jacques was probably not far from wrong. Most women he'd met who ran places for young women of distinction were of a markedly religious bent. Or at least they pretended to be, for it seemed to be a requirement of the families who entrusted their daughters to the care of such an establishment.

He took his hat off and knocked on the front door, nudging Jacques with his elbow until he also took his cap off. Leo was trying to smooth his hair into some semblance of order when the door opened.

Margaret stepped into the doorway, a smile on her face. "Hello, Leo, Jacques," she said, her voice sounding almost musical to Leo.

"Hello, Miss Margaret," Leo said, while Jacques smiled and nodded, amused at the way Leo, who normally was quite accomplished at casual conversation, seemed to become almost tongue-tied in the young woman's presence.

"There's someone I'd like you two to meet," Margaret said, stepping to the side and holding out her arm.

The figure that stepped up beside her in the door was big, standing almost six feet tall and with broad shoulders. Backlit as she was by the lanterns inside the house, her face could not at first be seen.

Jacques looked at Leo, and Leo could hear him gulp, as if in fear. The woman turned slightly, her face coming into view as the light shifted. She had coarse features, with a broad, flat nose that almost looked as if it'd been broken in a bar fight, with salt-and-pepper hair, a large mole on her left cheek that also had hair growing from it, and a sharp chin that jutted from under her nose like the bow of a particularly ugly ship.

Leo heard Jacques whisper, "Oh, no," to himself as he started to back off the porch.

Leo grabbed his arm and squeezed it to make him behave, trying his best to smile at the apparition in the doorway. "Good evening, I am Dr. Leo LeMat, and this is my friend, Jacques LeDieux."

The woman in the doorway stuck out her hand like a man, and when she spoke, her voice was low and harsh, also like a man's. "Good evening, sir."

Leo took her hand, noticing it was almost as big as his, while with his left arm he struggled to keep Jacques from bolting down the street. "And are you—?"

Margaret, sensing what he was about to say, interrupted. "Dr. LeMat, I'd like you to meet Madame Abigail Pringle, our house mistress."

Leo relaxed and heard Jacques let his breath out with a soft sigh. "Margaret has told us many nice things about you, Mrs. Pringle," Leo said, giving her hand a slight squeeze and bowing his head slightly, as good gentlemen were supposed to.

Pringle's thick lips spread in what might have been her attempt at a smile, though it did little to soften her features or to make her more feminine. "Won't you come in, gentlemen? Perhaps we might have a cup of tea before you leave for dinner."

She turned and led them inside without waiting for an answer, her stride long and her shoulders rolling with her gait like a man's. "I always like to meet the gentlemen who call on my ladies," Pringle continued as she walked toward a small table and chairs in the dining room, already set with a tea service.

Jacques looked around the immense living and sitting room, wondering where the young woman named Gretchen was. He felt he had already dodged one bullet and sincerely hoped Gretchen would be an improvement over Madame Pringle.

There were several young ladies sitting around the room in various places, some knitting or doing needlepoint, and all were trying to look at Jacques and Leo without being observed, but none were paying special attention.

"Ah, here is Gretchen now," Pringle said, as a small, petite woman walked out of the kitchen carrying a pot of tea. She had long, dark hair that fell to her shoulders, a slim but well-proportioned figure that the full dress with its ruffles and folds of material could not hide, and a face that rivaled Margaret's for sheer beauty.

Jacques stopped dead in his tracks, his mouth open and his eyes wide. "That . . . that is Gretchen?" he rasped, as though someone had their hands on his throat.

Margaret gave him a smile, as if she knew what he'd been thinking. "Jacques LeDieux, this is Gretchen Albright, my friend."

Gretchen's face blushed slightly and she gave a small curtsy, her dark brown eyes looking at Jacques with approval.

Jacques quickly stepped to her side and took the teapot from her, putting it on the table. He turned to her, gave a short bow, and took her hand, bringing it to his lips for a quick brush. "I am *very* pleased to meet you, Mademoiselle Gretchen," he said, his eyes fairly twinkling with his delight at her appearance.

Leo noticed Jacques's voice was much softer than usual, and his French accent slightly more pronounced when he spoke with Gretchen. Leo glanced upward. *Thank you, God*, he thought to himself. Perhaps the night would be as magical as he hoped it would be after all.

After they'd been seated at the Florentine restaurant, the only one in town Jacques thought worthy of dining at, Leo ordered wine for everyone and they sat chatting prior to ordering.

"Miss Abigail seems very nice," he commented to Margaret, noticing that Jacques could barely take his eyes off Gretchen long enough to taste his wine.

Margaret agreed. "She is exceptionally nice, though she does have a rather antiquated idea of how much modern women need to be protected from the world. It is as if she believes we are all small children who cannot get about in the city without her guidance."

"But, Maggie," Gretchen said, "not all of the girls are as self-sufficient as you are. Some of them truly need her to show them how young ladies should act."

"Perhaps," Margaret said politely, though it was

obvious she didn't share Gretchen's assessment of the other women in the boarding house.

Gretchen turned her lovely eyes on Jacques. "Maggie has told me about Mr. LeMat, Jacques, but she was very mysterious when talking about you. What do you do?"

Jacques answered, his eyes never leaving Gretchen's. "I manage Leo's affairs. I am in charge of cooking, making travel arrangements, and seeing that he does not forget to eat, things of that nature," he said with a deprecating smile, dipping his eyes modestly.

"So, you like to cook?" Gretchen asked.

"Jacques lives to cook, and he is quite excellent at it," Leo replied.

Gretchen smiled, staring at Jacques. "I, too, love to cook," she said. "Especially French food."

Jacques's face lit up. "*Bon!* We must compare recipes. Perhaps you can teach me something," he said, an admission Leo had never heard his friend make to anyone about his culinary talents.

"And what about you, Leo?" Margaret asked. "Have you found a subject for your painting?"

"As a matter of fact, I am in the process of doing a portrait of Judge Parker."

"Judge Parker, that barbarian?" Margaret asked, a look of disgust on her face.

"On the contrary," Leo said, somewhat taken aback by Margaret's reaction. "I found the judge to be most charming and conscientious concerning his duties."

"But how can you have any respect for a man who presides over that abomination he calls a jail?"

Leo spread his palms. "Well, I'll admit I haven't seen the jail yet. . . ."

"It's a veritable hell on earth," Margaret said. "The prisoners have a name for it, the Hell on the Border Jail."

Leo took a sip of his wine, wisely saying nothing when he saw how seriously Margaret felt about her subject.

"It's in the basement of the federal courthouse," she continued, leaning forward, her face flushed in her excitement, "and consists of two rooms with no light except what comes from underground windows and no outside ventilation. It was built for forty men, but last week there were over a hundred and ten men caged there like animals. The only opportunity for washing the men have is half a bucket of water in each cell, and it is so hot there the men throw water on the flagstone floors trying to cool it down, but it only makes the air heavy with steam and a suffocating stench that turns the stomach."

Trying to derail her, Leo poured some more wine into her glass, but she ignored his efforts. He glanced sideways at Gretchen, who only shrugged slightly as if used to Margaret's tirades on the subject.

"The jail is a piece of medieval barbarity, with no separation of prisoners by types of crimes. Why, a young boy convicted of stealing a piece of bread might be in the same cell with a convicted murderer."

As Margaret spoke, Gretchen touched Jacques's hand, sending electric shivers up his spine. "You can see that Margaret feels very strongly about such things," she whispered in his ear, causing the hair on the back of his neck to stir and his heart to pound.

He nodded, still unable to take his eyes off her. His nostrils quivered as he caught a faint scent of lilacs wafting from her skin.

"What excuse does the government of the United States have for the existence of this scandal?" Margaret asked.

Leo reached out and touched her arm. "I can see your point, Margaret, but to blame Judge Parker for the existence of the jail is not very fair. I hear he has petitioned the government to build a new, more humane jail and has even provided some of the funding for the project from his own pocket."

Margaret sat back in her chair and delicately wiped a slight sheen of sweat from her upper lip before taking a drink of the wine Leo had ordered.

"Yes, of course you're right," she admitted, "but I just cannot stand to see human beings treated so terribly."

To change the subject, Jacques picked up the menu lying by his side. "I believe it is time to order."

Gretchen again touched his hand. "Why don't you order for all of us, Jacques?"

Leo ducked his head to hide his smile. This woman certainly knew the way to Jacques's heart.

"Of course, Mademoiselle Gretchen," he said, holding his hand up and snapping his fingers to summon their waiter.

When their food arrived, everyone at the table smiled in anticipation. Jacques had ordered beef, sautéed in Burgundy sauce, asparagus smothered with hollandaise sauce, and candied carrots so sweet they tasted as if they'd been covered with brown sugar.

"This smells delicious," Margaret said, inhaling the aroma of the beef.

"If it has been prepared correctly," Jacques said, picking up his utensils, "you will not need a knife to cut it. A fork should be sufficient."

While they ate, Leo kept up a steady stream of conversation, trying his best to steer clear of any reference to topics he knew were dear to Margaret's heart.

Both Margaret and Gretchen were enthralled with their tales of their encounters with Wyatt Earp and Doc Holliday on Leo and Jacques's last trip out West.

Gretchen was particularly interested in how a man like Doc Holliday, suffering from consumption, could still practice dentistry.

Leo laughed and told her he had few clients, which was one of the reasons he made most of his living from playing cards and gambling.

Unfortunately, this brought on a minor tirade by Margaret about the evils of both gambling and drinking of spirits.

Jacques glanced at Gretchen and winked, while Leo just listened as if he agreed with every word.

Other than that, the dinner went remarkably well, and the four enjoyed a thoroughly delightful evening out on the town.

When they took the women home to Madam Pringle's boarding house, they parted with promises to get together again . . . soon.

As Leo and Jacques walked back to their hotel, Leo couldn't resist a jibe at his friend.

"So, I guess you changed your mind about women named Gretchen?" he asked.

Jacques pursed his lips, considering his reply. "No, not in general. Gretchen is and always will be a terrible name for a woman. However, my

Gretchen rises above the inequity of her name and is truly a beautiful specimen of womanhood."

"Does that mean you really do plan to see her again?" Leo asked.

Jacques looked astounded his friend would ask such a question. "Of course, *mon ami*. I would be a fool not to spend as much time in this wasteland as I can with such a beautiful lady."

"Well, she *is* interested in French cooking," Leo observed as they approached their hotel. "Perhaps you can get together and compare recipes."

"Perhaps," Jacques said, a slight smile on his face, "and perhaps, after a few more nights spent with Jacques LeDieux, she will be far more interested in French men than in French cooking."

# Chapter 11

After his lawyers arranged for Cherokee Bill, also known as Crawford Goldsby, to get a stay of execution pending his appeal, he was moved to the newly constructed jail adjacent to the federal courthouse. The new jail consisted of a three-story cage made of iron bars, with screen on the floors. Judge Parker had decreed that the most infamous convicts be on the first floor, with the severity of the criminals decreasing on the higher floors. Cherokee Bill was on the first floor, called "Murderers' Row" by the prisoners.

Cherokee Bill was sitting in a corner, idly shuffling some playing cards the guards had let him keep, when another prisoner, Henry Star, sauntered over.

"Hey, Bill," Star said, "I heard you was in here. How're they hangin'?"

Bill looked up, a sneer on his face. "They ain't hangin' all that well, Henry," he answered. "I been in here so long I 'bout forgot what my woman looks like.''

Star squatted on his haunches in front of Bill. "I know the feelin'."

"What'd they git you for?" Bill asked, cutting the cards and dealing a hand to Star.

"They said I kilt Deputy Marshal Floyd Wilson."

Bill's lips curled in a lopsided grin. "Did you?"

Star looked around to see if anyone could hear. Satisfied they were alone, he grinned back. " 'Course I did. The sumbitch was tryin' to arrest me. But my flathead lawyers have managed to get me an appeal to the U.S. Supreme Court, so I'm not supposed to tell anybody that."

"I'm waitin' on an appeal, too," Bill said. "I guess the courts don't much like the Hangin' Judge's record if they're willin' to check up on all his convictions."

Star shook his head. "It ain't that, it's these damned lawyers. They could sell mud to a pig wallowin' in it."

"Good thing for us, huh?" Bill asked.

"Damn right," Star replied.

They continued to play cards, betting their day's rations of tobacco on the hands.

After a while, Bill got to his feet and walked to the wall under one of the windows too high to look out and stood there, gazing up at the weak rays of sunlight filtering through the bars.

"You all right, Bill?" Star asked.

"I can't stand much more of this. I gotta get outta here," Bill growled, his eyes wild.

"I heard the guards searched the place a while back and found nine .45 cartridges and an old .45 revolver hid in the bathroom. Those yours?"

Bill nodded without turning to look at Star. "Yeah, they *were*. Now I got to find me another way to break out."

Star grimaced. "I don't see how that's possible. This place is built pretty solid."

Bill glanced at the other end of the cell, where a man wearing the white coat and pants of a trustee was mopping the floor. "See that man over there?" he asked.

Star looked. "Yeah."

"That's Sherman Vann. My woman, Maggie Glass, paid him a handsome sum to smuggle me in another pistol."

Star's eyebrows lifted in surprise. "You mean he did it?"

Bill grinned. "Maggie can be mighty persuasive when she wants to be. That's how they caught me in the first place, when I went over to see her an' get my ashes hauled."

"What'd you do with it? I hear the guards are watchin' you real close."

"I got it hid in a hole in the wall of my cell, covered over with the mud that's always on the floor in here."

"They gonna kill you if you try again, Bill," Star said.

"That's my worry, Henry," Bill growled, his voice suddenly turning hard and making the hair on the back of Star's neck stir. He thought to himself it was like looking Death straight in the face to cross Cherokee Bill.

Bill glanced around to make sure no one was within earshot. "You just keep your mouth shut 'bout what I tole you an' you might just live to find out about your appeal."

It was close to seven o'clock in the evening and time for the prisoners to be returned to their individual cells. During the day, they were allowed to roam the entire cell block area in order to get some exercise, but at night they were put back in their cells.

Guards Campbell Eoff and Lawrence Keating entered Murderers' Row, while night guards Will Lawson, Bras Parker, and William McConnel, who'd just come on duty, waited outside the cell block.

Eoff began making his rounds, locking the cells

as the prisoners went into them. When he got to the cell next to Cherokee Bill's, he had trouble inserting the key. He bent and looked at the lock. Someone had inserted wadded-up paper in the keyhole.

"Hey, Larry," he called to Keating, "somethin's wrong here. Somebody's been messin' with this lock."

Cherokee Bill leaped from his cell. In his right hand was a pistol, the hammer pulled back and the barrel pointing at the two guards.

"Get your hands up, you two!" he shouted.

Keating whirled around, going for the pistol on his right hip, and Bill shot him in the stomach. Keating grabbed his gut with a loud grunt and doubled over, falling to his knees.

Eoff took off at a dead run up the corridor, bending over to make himself less of a target.

Bill walked after him, squeezing off four shots as other prisoners ducked for cover from the lead slugs ricocheting off the stone walls of the prison.

George Pearce, who'd helped Bill plan the break, was in the next cell. He kicked a small table in his cell over, bent down and wrenched one of the legs of the table free. He bounded out of his cell, also chasing Eoff down the corridor, brandishing his table leg like a club, yelling wildly as some other prisoners, terrified for their lives, screamed for help from the guards.

As Eoff dove around a bend in the corridor, guards McConnel, Parker, and Lawson stuck pistols through the iron bars and opened fire on the marauding prisoners, forcing them back toward their cells.

Will Lawson slipped into the cell block and made his way toward Keating, who lay at the foot of the stairs in a pool of his own blood.

Lawson crept down the corridor until he could squat next to the wounded guard. He reached down and picked up his pistol off the floor and was startled when Keating rolled over and grabbed his arm.

"Kill the dog, Will. He has killed me," Keating groaned, blood leaking from his lips. Then he gasped, his lungs making bubbling sounds as he squeezed Lawson's arm, and died.

Will Lawson shook the man's shoulders, but Keating was beyond feeling it.

Leo was gathering up his sketch pad and charcoal and putting them in his valise, for the evening session of court had just ended. He'd gained more respect for Judge Parker's restraint after sitting in the courtroom while a lawyer representing two men who'd gotten drunk and killed a couple of passersby argued that his clients should be set free because they didn't "mean" to kill anyone.

Leo's mother, who was a cousin of the infamous

Younger brothers and who always said Leo got the "dark" side of his nature from her, nevertheless had taught him one must always accept the responsibility for one's actions. Leo agreed, knowing that in a country based on freedom like the United States, personal responsibility was a must.

He'd been secretly glad when Judge Parker, who evidently felt as he did, shut the two killers' lawyer down with a few well-chosen and very sarcastic remarks before sentencing them to ten years in the territorial prison. It seemed to Leo that Parker had a good balance of compassion for the men he sentenced to die on a daily basis mixed with a healthy respect for the need for them to be responsible for their actions, no matter the provocation. All in all, he figured, if the judge was truly as bent on hanging men as his reputation said, he could easily have sentenced the two men to the gallows. The fact that he didn't show, he bought at least some of the argument that the killings had been accidental.

*I'd better hurry,* Leo thought after glancing at the Regulator clock on the wall and seeing the time. Jacques and Gretchen were supposed to accompany him and Margaret to the Gaslight Playhouse tonight to see some traveling players in a stage production. The leading lady was supposed to be the next Lillie Langtry, and Leo was looking forward to seeing if she lived up to her billing.

The booming of gunfire rang out and seemed

to be coming from the jail area next door to the courtroom.

Judge Parker stopped on his way to his chambers and turned, a horrified expression on his face. "What the hell was that?" he asked Deputy Marshal Heck Bruner, who'd just finished testifying against a murderer named Shorty Matthews.

"Sounds like somthin' goin' on over at the jail," Bruner replied, cocking his head, his hand unconsciously falling to the butt of the pistol on his hip.

"Get over there and find out!" Parker shouted.

"Come on, Cap'n," Bruner said to Captain Berry, who was standing nearby.

As the two men ran out the door, Leo dropped his valise and followed, reaching in his coat to make sure his Baby LeMat was ready for action.

When they reached the jailhouse, they saw Lawson driven back by gunfire from Cherokee Bill, who'd managed to reach the safety of his cell, where he commanded a view of the corridor and could fire without danger of being hit himself.

"What the hell's goin' on?" Bruner asked as he crouched next to Lawson, Parker, and McConnel, with Berry and Leo standing behind him looking over his shoulder.

"It's a standoff, Heck," Will Lawson replied, looking back over his shoulder at the marshal. "We got Cherokee Bill trapped in his cell where he can't go nowhere, but he's got a clear line of sight down the corridor an' we can't get in the cell block, neither."

Occasionally, Bill would fire his pistol and when the guards returned fire, the murderer would gobble like a turkey and yell insults.

The marshals glanced at each other, their eyebrows raised. "What's that son of a bitch doin'?" Bruner asked, his lips curled in a grin.

"Hell if I know," Lawson replied, shaking his head. "Everbody knows Cherokee Bill is crazy."

After about fifteen minutes, Leo noticed the body of Keating lying in the corridor halfway down toward where Bill was crouched. "There's a wounded man in there," he said. "I'm a doctor. Let me see if I can get to him."

"I think he's already dead," Will Lawson said.

"Still, if there's a chance, I'd like to try," Leo replied.

Bruner shrugged. "Go on, mister. It's your funeral."

Leo crouched down as low as he could and ran down the corridor, ducking even further as two bullets from Bill ricocheted off the stone walls of the jail and buzzed by inches from his head.

When he got to Keating, he dragged him up against the wall to gain some cover and checked the pulse in his neck. There was no heartbeat. It was clear the man was dead. Leo glanced around to see if there were any way he could get the drop on Bill. The man was holed up in there like it was a fortress, Leo thought, craning his neck to get a better view of Bill's cell.

Suddenly, Bill stuck his head up, saw Leo, and fired without aiming. The slug slammed into the stone next to Leo's face, sending slivers of rock flying, lacerating his cheek and barely missing his right eye.

Leo threw himself flat on the floor, hiding himself partially behind the dead guard's body. *He's past caring if a couple more bullets hit him*, Leo reasoned to himself. He raised his head slightly and looked around at the cell block, noticing the rest of the prisoners were hunkered down, hiding under their bunks with their hands over their ears. A couple were staring wide-eyed at Leo, wondering what he was going to do next.

Leo stretched out and lay on his belly behind the body of the guard, his pistol in his hand, waiting for a chance at Bill.

"Cherokee Bill," Heck Bruner yelled from the end of the room, "you can't get out! Throw down your gun and come out with your hands up!"

Through the small windows of the jail, a crowd that'd gathered outside could be heard yelling, "Lynch him! String the bastard up!"

Bill yelled back, "I didn't want to kill Keating! I wanted my liberty. Damn a man that won't fight for his liberty! If I hadn't shot him, he would've shot me."

Henry Star, who was watching the drama from his cell on the west side of the cell block, hollered, "Marshal, if you promise not to shoot Bill, I'll get his gun."

Bruner looked at Captain Berry. He'd never heard of such a thing, but they really didn't have any choice. It was either that or wait for days and try to starve Bill out.

"All right, Star. You can give it a try. If Bill throws his gun down, we won't shoot." He looked around at the guards. "Hold your fire, men. Give Star a chance," he called, holding up his hand.

Star eased out of his cell and made his way to Bill's cell, calling out to him who it was so Bill wouldn't shoot him as he entered.

Leo listened and could hear Star talking in a low voice. "Bill, you got to give it up. There ain't no way they're gonna let you outta here 'cept on a board, full of holes."

"I ain't done yet, Henry," Bill said and loosed off a couple more shots and gobbled again.

"Bill, what do you want?" Star asked, ducking when Bill fired. "You might get a couple more guards, but they're sure as hell gonna kill you sooner or later."

Bill shrugged and began to punch out his empty brass.

"Come on, Bill. Your lawyers are workin' on an appeal. Give 'em a chance to get you outta here the easy way."

Leo, hearing the exchange, added, "He's got a point, Bill. It won't do you any good to win an appeal if you're dead and buried."

Bill raised his head to stare at Leo, who was still behind Keating's body, only his eyes showing.

"Who the hell are you?" Bill called.

"I'm the man that's going to put a bullet in your gut if you don't throw that pistol down and come on out of there," Leo replied, letting Bill see the twin barrels of his Baby LeMat.

Bill sat back down in his cell, his back against the stone wall, and hung his head, staring at the empty pistol in his hand.

After a few minutes, he sighed deeply. "You two got a point, Henry," Bill said, evidently forgetting he'd just killed a prison guard in his escape attempt and had absolutely no chance of winning an appeal to his death sentence.

He turned to stare out the window at the faint glow of sunlight, as if wondering if he'd ever see it again without bars between him and the sky.

He finally handed Star the weapon then climbed up on his bunk and lay back down, waiting for them to come get him.

Star yelled, "I've got the gun, and I'm comin' out. Don't shoot."

He walked out of Bill's cell, stopping for a moment as he saw Leo draw a bead on his chest with his pistol.

"Come on out," Leo said, the barrel of his gun unwavering.

Star continued down the corridor to the cell block door with the pistol hanging from his finger by the trigger guard, where Heck Bruner grabbed the Colt and told Star to get back in his cell.

The guards then rushed up the corridor and surrounded Bill, who lay apparently unconcerned on his bunk. They jerked him to his feet and put him in shackles and chains while they searched the rest of his cell.

Leo got to his feet, took a last look at the dead man, Keating, and walked slowly out of the jail, hoping he wasn't too late for the stage show.

As he walked by the marshals, Bruner gave him a look, tipped his hat and smiled, and then he turned his attention back to Cherokee Bill.

He later heard, after Bill was again sentenced to hang and was taken to the gallows, that the murderer, upon seeing hangman George Maledon standing next to the rope, grinned and turned his face up to let the sun shine on his face.

When Maledon slipped the rope around his neck, he asked Bill, "You got any last words?"

Bill shook his head, his grin still in place, and said in a steady voice, "This is as good a day to die as any."

# Chapter 12

Leo brushed at his coat to get the jailhouse dust and dirt off as he hurried up Main Street to meet Jacques and the ladies for dinner and a night at the theater. He forced his mind away from the image of the dead guard to more pleasant things, such as the way Margaret would look dressed for an evening out on the town.

He hadn't felt this way about a woman since his wife had died years before, and he smiled to himself at the way the prospect of being in her company made his heart beat fast and his stomach flutter.

*Damn, Leo*, he thought, *you're acting like a kid who's courting for the first time*. He tried to be adult and to examine his feelings for the woman he'd just met a few days earlier, but, as with all matters of the heart, logic had very little to do with the way she made him feel. Her beauty, her intellect, and her passion for all things important to her made her more attractive to him than anyone he'd met in many years.

It'd been a long time since he'd thought about the implications of falling in love and what it would do to his life. As he walked, he began to wonder if he was at last ready to marry again and settle down, if the wanderlust that had infected him since his wife's passing would abate or if he would continue to feel the need to travel the country and see what was over the next hill.

He also had to consider what Margaret would want out of a life with him. Would she be content to travel with him, exploring new areas and meeting new and exciting people? Or, would she prefer to settle down in San Antonio or New Orleans and lead the life of the wife of a famous painter?

*You're getting way ahead of yourself,* he thought, wondering if Margaret's feelings for him were as strong as his were for her. Perhaps their upcoming meeting would shed some light on her feelings and give him a clue as to what to expect if things progressed as he hoped they would.

When he reached their hotel, he found Jacques and the women in the dining room, already eating.

Jacques looked up when Leo entered and pointedly glanced at his watch. "Good evening, Leo," he said. "We were beginning to wonder if you'd found something else more exciting to do tonight instead of dining with us," Jacques said, a glint in his eye as if he knew nothing would have kept Leo from his appointment with the beautiful Margaret.

"Hello, Leo," Margaret said, a slight blush appearing on her cheeks as she dropped her eyes.

"Good evening," Leo answered, signaling to the waiter as he pulled a chair out and took his seat. "I'm sorry I'm late, but just as the court was ending, there was an attempted jailbreak next door."

Jacques's eyes narrowed. "We heard the shots, but couldn't tell where they came from. We thought it might have been some cowboys letting off steam."

"What happened, Leo?" Margaret asked. "Was anyone hurt in the gunfight?"

Leo's manner became more serious. "Yes. One of the guards, a man named Keating, was killed."

Margaret's hand went to her mouth and she groaned. "Larry Keating?"

"I believe that was his name," Leo said, noticing how her face paled. "Why? Did you know him?"

She nodded, tears brimming her eyes. "Yes. I occasionally take jelly and bread to the prisoners, and Mr. Keating was always very nice to me. Moreover, he seemed to genuinely care for the plight of the prisoners and tried to make things as easy for them as he could."

Jacques's face darkened. "And that is how they

repay his kindness? By shooting him down like a dog?"

Margaret glanced at Jacques. "Oh, Jacques, do not believe I have any illusions about the type of men who are incarcerated in the jail just because I am against capital punishment. I know that most of them have done horrible things to be put there. It's just that I don't believe two wrongs make a right. Don't you see, if we kill them, then we are no better than they are."

Jacques shook his head, his jaw set in the way Leo knew meant Margaret was in for an argument.

"No, mademoiselle, I do not," Jacques said, wiping his lips with his napkin. "If I am on the street and I see a mad dog who is about to bite someone, and I shoot him to protect them, then I do not feel I am also the mad dog."

Margaret wagged her head. "That's not the same thing," she said.

"Oh, but it is," Jacques replied, leaning forward. "Most of the men in that jail are much worse than mad dogs, for they at least have had the opportunity to learn the difference between right and wrong, even if they choose to ignore it. And, unlike the poor dog, they not only bite, they kill."

"Then lock them away, but don't lower yourself to their level by committing murder. The old argument that the fear of hanging will keep men from killing has never been shown to be correct. All of these men on death row knew they would be hanged if caught, and yet they still committed the crimes for which they are condemned."

"Miss Margaret, prisons are not perfect places as you know. Quite often these bad men escape from jail and kill again, but as I've said before, once hanged, they can never again take a life."

Leo, to change the subject, called the waiter over and said he'd have whatever the others were having and ordered another bottle of wine.

"Jacques, Margaret," he said reasonably, "good people can disagree about such things, but we mustn't let it ruin our night out. One thing I've learned in my advanced years is not to talk politics or religion over dinner, for it spoils both the appetite and the evening."

Gretchen, who'd been silent so far, cocked an eyebrow at Leo. "Oh, Leo, I don't think your years are so advanced."

Margaret lost her serious look and grinned. "Nor do I, Leo," she added, her comment bringing a bright red blush to her cheeks.

Jacques cleared his throat, forcing himself to grin and try to lighten the mood. "Well, you ladies are both wrong. Leo is even older than he looks. Why, he's almost old enough to be my father."

"Then this old man may just have to teach you some manners," Leo said in mock anger, "like your father should have done when you were a pup."

Jacques smiled for the ladies. "I told you he is older, but I did not say wiser."

The waiter forestalled Leo's reply by arriving with the extra bottle of wine and his food.

Leo uncorked the bottle and refilled glasses all around, then he offered a toast. "To new friends and new adventures," he said, holding his glass high.

The others did the same, and they all drank.

"Now, Leo, you must hurry and eat your food," Jacques said, glancing at a clock on the wall. "Your meddling in the affairs of the sheriff has caused us to be late for the next show at the theater."

After the show at the Gaslight Theater was over, Leo and Jacques and the two women stopped by a local diner for some coffee and cognac.

Leo noticed Jacques and Gretchen had their heads together, sharing a quiet laugh.

Leo nudged Margaret and she smiled at the antics of Jacques and Gretchen, who were acting like two teenagers out on a picnic. "What's so funny?" Leo asked, sipping coffee strengthened by a dollop of cognac.

Jacques looked up from staring into Gretchen's eyes. "I told Gretchen that the woman in the stage play tonight looked a lot like what I had imagined she would look like when Margaret set up our meeting."

Leo chuckled, while Margaret looked puzzled. The woman, a famous player, weighed over two hundred pounds, with huge, pendulous breasts and a face that would better suit a horse. She was famous for a rich contralto voice that rang from the rafters of any theater, no matter how large. Leo knew from attending many operas and stage plays that a large frame was to be expected in such performers, but the image of the illustrious player greeting Jacques on their first dinner outing was very humorous.

He finally had to explain to Margaret that Jacques had been convinced the woman she wanted him to meet was going to be enormously fat and ugly, and how pleasantly surprised he'd been over Gretchen's beauty.

When both Margaret and Gretchen covered their mouths and giggled, Leo again asked why.

"Gretchen thought much like Jacques and almost refused to go out with us, being equally sure he would turn out to have only a modicum of teeth and no personality whatsoever," Margaret explained as Gretchen blushed and laid her hand gently on Jacques's arm. "She, too, was very pleasantly surprised at how Jacques turned out to be," Margaret added.

"That is only because I forced him to bathe, for the first time in weeks," Leo said with a laugh.

"That's not true!" Jacques protested. "I bathe regularly, at least once a week whether I need to or not."

As the evening wore down, Leo couldn't help but think how wonderfully things had turned out on this trip to Arkansas. Both he and Jacques had met beautiful women they were infatuated with, and soon Leo's thoughts turned to the possibility of marriage.

While Margaret sipped her coffee and cognac and traded quips with Gretchen and Jacques, Leo sat back and wondered about the changes in his life marriage might bring. Margaret could indeed be a woman he felt he could share the rest of his life with and never again have a dull moment.

Suddenly, Margaret put her cup down and looked at Gretchen. "Oh, look at the time," she said, glancing at a Regulator clock on the wall, which showed a quarter to midnight. "We've got to get home and pack for our trip tomorrow, Gretchen," she said.

"Trip?" Leo asked.

"Yes. Gretchen and I are traveling on the train tomorrow night to Adair, in Indian Territory. Carrie Nation is going to be there and we are going to have a march protesting the selling of strong spirits to young cowboys who aren't old enough to know better."

Jacques caught Gretchen's eye. "That is some pretty rough country for two ladies to travel to alone. Would you like us to accompany you?" he asked. "That is, if Leo can tear himself away from his painting of Judge Parker for a day or two."

Margaret shook her head, smiling. "Now, Jacques. This is the nineteenth century and Gretchen and I are perfectly capable of taking care of ourselves."

"But . . ." Jacques started to protest.

Gretchen placed her hand on his arm and stood up. "Thank you for the offer, Jacques," she said, "it's very gallant of you, but Margaret and I will be just fine. Besides, you and Leo have your work here to keep you busy until we return."

Leo stared at Margaret, a feeling of dread coursing through his heart at the thought of being separated from her, even for a few days. "It will seem like an empty town without you here to share it with me," he said in a low voice, his eyes boring into hers.

She put her arm in his and squeezed it tightly. "Oh, don't you worry about that, Leo. I have a feeling we're going to have plenty of time together," she said, making Leo's heart flutter and a funny feeling appear in the pit of his stomach.

Leo paid their bill and he and Jacques walked

the ladies to their rooming house, their arms intertwined and their shoulders touching. After seeing
them safely into the house, he and Jacques continued toward their hotel alone.

As they walked, Leo softly hummed tunes from
the stage play they'd attended.

Jacques glanced at him, a serious look on his
face. *"Mon ami,"* he said, "I think you are having
thoughts similar to mine about these young
women."

"Oh?" Leo asked, though he knew full well
what Jacques was referring to.

*"Oui,* thoughts of finally settling down and
stopping this traveling to desolate regions to paint
desperados and lawmen. Thoughts of a house
filled once again with the laughter of small children and the smell of home cooking."

Leo looked at Jacques, surprised that his feelings were so transparent. "And you, my friend,
what do you think of such matters?"

"I, too, have had these thoughts, Leo." He
glanced into Leo's eyes. "I was hoping, if you
agreed, that a double wedding might be possible."

Leo laughed and clapped Jacques on the back.
"I would be honored, Jacques. Have you mentioned this to Gretchen?"

"No, I wanted to hear your thoughts on the
matter first."

"I think, if the lady in question is dumb enough

to accept your offer, you will be the second luckiest man in the world."

Jacques grinned. "Second only to you if Miss Margaret accepts your proposal?" he asked, a grin showing his teeth white in the moonlight.

"Exactly!" Leo responded.

# Chapter 13

Judge Isaac Parker stood before a second-story window overlooking the stone-walled courtyard around Fort Smith, his hands clasped behind his back. His wife Mary was standing behind him, watching him stare out of the window.

"Four more conscienceless men gone to eternity," he said quietly, watching four black-hooded bodies swing gently in the air from ropes tied to a beam above the gallows platform. "They gave me no choice. They were guilty."

"You grieve too much over it, my darling," Mary said. "It is your duty, as unpleasant as it is. You most certainly cannot set them free and the jail is already full to overflowing with men who've committed lesser crimes. You must believe you have no choice in the matter."

"My critics grow louder by the day," he said in a weary voice, turning to stand behind his desk, the window at his back. "The Supreme Court is

155

overturning more and more of my decisions. Cruel as they have said I am, they forget the utterly hardened character of the men I deal with. They forget that in my jurisdiction alone, sixty-five deputy marshals were murdered in the discharge of their duty."

He sat down at his desk and put his head in his hands. "The good ladies who carry flowers and jellies to criminals mean well. There is no doubt of that. But what mistaken goodness: sincere pity and charity, sadly misdirected. They see the convict alone, perhaps chained to his cell. They forget the crime he perpetrated and the family he made husbandless and fatherless by his assassin work." He stared up at his wife. "If only they spent as much of their pity on the victims as they do on the perpetrators, perhaps then I'd have more belief in what they say."

"You must put it behind you, Isaac."

"I have done what I can to silence the hounds on my heels. I wrote *The Saint Louis Globe-Democrat*. I said that during the twenty years that I have engaged in administering the law here, the contest has been one between civilization and the savagery represented by the intruding criminal class. The fault lies with the laxity of the courts, and the Supreme Court's tendency to concern itself with the flimsiest technicalities. Murders are on the increase. I attribute the increase to the Supreme

Court. The murderer has a long breathing spell before his case comes before the Supreme Court, and the conviction may be quashed upon the smallest thing. The Supreme Court never touches upon the merits of the case," he finished, shaking his head.

"Let it rest, darling. You know you haven't been feeling well lately," she said, stepping around the desk to stand at his side with her hand on his shoulder.

He placed his hand over hers and gave it a pat to show his gratitude for her concern. "An interesting fellow in my courtroom today. He was sketching my likeness. His name is Dr. Leo LeMat. He is a surgeon who is also a portrait painter who wishes to paint me. . . ." He raised his eyebrows at her and grinned. "And he is also a very accomplished pistolman."

She gave a low chuckle. "A surgeon, a painter, and a pistolman . . . my goodness, dear. He sounds quite accomplished."

Parker nodded. "Oh, he is. In fact, I've hired him in one instance to assist some of my marshals in bringing down a gang of criminals. He helped to halt an attempted jailbreak." He smiled deprecatingly at Mary. "What will you do with a portrait of me, my dear?"

"Hang it in the sitting room, of course. I hope this man is capable of capturing your strength of character on canvas," Mary said, leaning over to give him a quick buss on the cheek.

"At times like these I feel I have no strength of any kind, sweet wife," he said, leaning into her kiss. "I received a letter today informing me that the Supreme Court has overturned two more of my death sentences for criminals who surely deserved to hang."

"There is nothing more you can do, Isaac."

"A higher court has bound my hands. I have enemies in high places, it would seem."

"You can be confident that you have done your best to serve the law," Mary said, staring into his eyes.

He wondered if she could tell he'd been weeping after the hanging. It still pained him to the very depths of his soul to hang a man, no matter how grievous his crimes. He changed the subject. "I invited Dr. LeMat up to our quarters for a cup of tea. He should be here around five o'clock. Would you be so kind as to brew a pot of tea for us?"

"Of course, my dear. I'll get a fire going in the stove. I'm looking forward to meeting this unusual man with so many different . . . skills."

A rap on the upstairs door brought Judge Parker to his feet. He went to the door and opened it.

Dr. LeMat stood at the threshold, dressed in his black suit and stovepipe boots. He took off his flat-brim hat and offered his hand.

"Good to see you again, Dr. LeMat," Parker said, taking the offered handshake. "Please come in. Mary is making tea."

LeMat walked through the door. "I smell a wonderful smell, a good tea, an orange pekoe perhaps."

"You'll have to ask Mary. Take a chair. I noticed you today in my court making your preliminary drawings. However, I found it odd that you did not attend the hangings."

LeMat took a leather-bound chair. "I've seen quite enough death, Judge. I don't find it a suitable spectator event. I understand that those men needed to be hung for their crimes; however, it wasn't a thing I cared to see."

"How well I understand, Dr. LeMat. I feel duty-bound to watch the men I've sentenced to death go to their final reward, but it is not a pleasant pastime." He slumped in a chair across from LeMat's and loosened his string tie.

LeMat seemed to be admiring the bookshelves lining the sitting room, shelves filled with classics, bound legal codes, and a sizeable collection of poetry. Parker glanced at Lord Byron's *Hours of Idleness*, one of his favorites.

"I've finished my preliminary sketches, Judge," LeMat said. "When you have the time, I'd like to start work on canvas."

"This Saturday will be fine," Parker said. "When no court is in session."

"What time should I arrive?"

"Let's make it ten o'clock. The light should be good up here when Mary opens the curtains."

"Agreed," LeMat replied. "I'm looking forward to it. I've read a great deal about you, about your appointment by President Grant and the time you spent in St. Louis. All this helps me develop a character in oils. The eyes are windows into a man's soul. Once I frame your face, I'll go to work on your eyes. I must capture them first and build your portrait around them in order to produce a satisfactory result."

Parker chuckled. "How odd, that a man who uses a gun with skill can be so sensitive about his painting."

"I had a good teacher. George Catlin may be this country's most renowned portraitist. I was privileged to study under him in Pennsylvania a few years ago."

"I've heard of him. He painted Indians in the West, if I remember correctly."

"He captured their free spirits," LeMat agreed. "A very difficult task with oils."

Mary came into the room carrying a silver tray with a china tea service on it. She smiled when she saw Dr. LeMat.

LeMat came to his feet as Parker said, "This is my wife, Mary. Without her I would be utterly lost."

"Pleased to meet you, Mrs. Parker," LeMat said as Mary put down her tray on a dark oak coffee table. Then he bowed politely.

Mary appeared to blush slightly. "Thank you, Dr. LeMat. My husband has told me about you. I understand you will begin a portrait of Isaac."

"As soon as possible. We've agreed on Saturday morning for a beginning."

Mary began pouring tea into delicate white china cups. "Is it possible to purchase this portrait when you're finished?" she asked.

The question seemed to throw LeMat off stride. "I had hoped to add it to my personal collection, Mrs. Parker. Opportunities such as these are very rare. I'm sorry, but the portrait most likely wouldn't be for sale."

"Of course," Mary said. She handed LeMat a cup. "Sugar and cream are on the tray. I'm afraid I'm fresh out of lemons."

"Thank you," LeMat said. "Sugar and cream will be fine for me."

Parker gazed thoughtfully out a window for a

moment. "Would you agree to hire your gun again, Dr. LeMat? I'm dangerously short of deputies right now."

"Not on a long-term basis, Judge. However, if anything does happen while I'm here, I'll give it serious consideration."

"Good enough," Parker said, taking the cup of sweetened tea Mary offered him. "Let's hope nothing does happen, although I hear rumblings regarding one of the gangs near Tallequah. It may amount to nothing."

LeMat tasted his tea. "Delicious. Orange pekoe, just as I thought."

"I'm curious, Dr. LeMat," Mary began. "My husband tells me that you are a physician. What kept you from following such a wonderful profession?"

LeMat cast his eyes to the floor. "I lost my wife giving birth to our daughter. I used everything I'd been taught in the healing arts, and yet . . . I felt helpless."

"Enough, Mary," Parker said gently. "It is obvious this is a deeply personal matter."

"I'm sorry, Dr. LeMat," Mary said. "I didn't know . . ."

"It's quite all right, Mrs. Parker. I try not to think about it now. My daughter attends a boarding school in New Orleans. I visit her as often as I can."

"I understand," Mary said. "We have two sons. They are away visiting relatives in St. Louis and I miss them terribly."

LeMat seemed eager to change the subject. "I found your instructions to the jury today very interesting . . . different."

Parker smiled. "My jury instructions are virtually always the same." He leaned back in his chair and stared at the ceiling while he recited, "Gentlemen, the very power and majesty of the government and this law is in your hands. While it is not there in burning letters over the door, see to it that the maxim that no guilty man shall escape and no innocent man shall be punished shall be verified in this case, as it should be in every case. You will retire and make your verdict."

"A charge few honest men could ignore," LeMat observed as he sipped more tea. "Not too sympathetic toward either side."

"Sympathy should not be reserved wholly for the criminal. I believe in standing on the right side of the innocent . . . quiet, peaceful, law-abiding citizens. Is there no sympathy for them? At present, there seems to be a criminal wave sweeping over the country, the like of which I have never seen before. I feel it is at least partly due to the laxity of the courts. Liberty and life are precious unless those in authority have sense and spirit enough to defend them under the law."

"Well said, Judge. I wholeheartedly agree. And the final words you spoke to the condemned man today showed your compassion for him."

When Mary glanced at him, Parker explained, "I said, 'May God, whose laws you have broken and before whose tribunal you must then appear, have mercy on your soul.' I feel that while no one can claim that swift and sure punishment has slowed crime, this remains a side issue. The goal of the justice system is merely to punish the guilty. Since rehabilitation of criminals has been proven again and again a dismal failure, retribution should be the only purpose of punishment."

LeMat paused a moment, thinking. "Sometimes, even the legal system can't seek the needed retribution. Quite often, this is an occasion when a gun is called for."

"Thus the need for deputy marshals who know how to use a gun, Dr. LeMat. Far too many times, a gun is all these criminals understand."

As Parker spoke, Leo noticed a fine sweat break out on his forehead, though the room was far from hot. After a moment, Parker stood up. "Excuse me, Dr. LeMat, I must use the outhouse."

As the judge walked away, he shook his head. "It seems I spend half my time there these days," he mumbled to himself.

After he left, Leo spoke to Mary. "Has the judge been ill?"

She looked up, a worried expression on her face. "Yes, but don't tell him I told you. He has been losing weight, and he rises six or seven times a night to use the chamber pot."

"Does he get weak and break out in a sweat often, especially after eating rich foods?"

Mary looked surprised. "Why, yes, he does. How did you know?"

Parker walked back into the room, still adjusting his pants. "Have you been bothering the doctor with your worries about my health, Mary?" he chided.

As she dropped her eyes, Leo said, "She has answered some questions I put to her, Judge. From what she told me, I think you may have diabetes mellitus."

"What?"

"It is called sugar diabetes by lay folk," Leo explained. "It is a condition in which your body cannot absorb the sugar in your diet."

"Is it dangerous?" Mary asked, looking more worried than before.

"Yes," Leo said softly. "Untreated, it may lead to blindness, or the forced amputation of your lower limbs."

Parker took a deep breath. "And what is the treatment?"

"Until recently, there was none. However, a Dr. Bouchardat noticed a diminution of sugar in the urine of his diabetic patients during rationing of food in Paris while under siege during the Franco-Prussian War."

Parker glanced at his wife, a slight smile on his face. "I might have known, dear, it is your magnificent cooking that is to blame for my malady."

Leo grinned, thinking it was evident these two loved each other very much. "As a matter of fact," he added, "a Dr. Catoni advises keeping diabetic patients under lock and key to make them adhere to his diet plan."

"I'm quite sure that won't be necessary for the judge," Mary said. "If you will be so kind as to give me a list of what is permissible, I will make sure Isaac eats nothing else."

Leo nodded and arose. "I will make the list as soon as I get back to my hotel." He hesitated, then added, "Oh, and Mrs. Parker . . ."

"Yes?"

"Even though my portrait of the judge is not for sale, I will do a little extra work on my preliminary sketches and they should look quite presentable to hang in your sitting room."

"Thank you, Dr. LeMat," she said, extending her hand. "For everything."

# Chapter 14

As the Union Pacific train pulled into the outskirts of Adair, in northeastern Indian Territory, Margaret began putting away the basket of fried chicken and fruit Leo and Jacques had presented her and Gretchen with on their leaving Fort Smith.

Gretchen wiped her mouth with a silk handkerchief Jacques had given her to use as a napkin. "It was certainly nice of the men to give us this basket of food for our trip," she said.

Margaret agreed. "Yes. I'm afraid it will be too late to dine by the time we get our bags and arrange suitable lodging, if there is any to be had."

Several gunshots rang out, startling Margaret, making her drop the basket on the floor.

"Goodness," Gretchen exclaimed. "What was that?"

Margaret leaned over to peer out the window, but couldn't see much through the sooty glass.

She reached up and lowered the window, sticking her head out to see what was going on.

She saw a group of men run out of the depot and break into two groups. Several men jumped in the cab of the train, holding guns on the engineer, while another group climbed aboard a nearby wagon and backed the horses up to the express car.

She ducked her head back inside just as the conductor came running down the aisle, a pistol in his hand. "Keep your heads down, ladies," he called as he hurried by. "They're robbin' the train!"

In spite of his warning, Margaret stuck her head back out, intent on watching the proceedings.

"What's happening?" Gretchen asked, leaning over, trying to see past Margaret's head.

"The robbers are pointing a pistol at a man in the express car," she said, "trying to make him open the door, I suspect."

She continued to watch as three men jumped inside the express car, apparently in an attempt to have someone inside open the safe.

Soon, men began unloading it, throwing bags of coins and money into the wagon parked just outside the door.

Margaret ducked as more shots rang out when guards in the smoker opened fire on the bandits.

The outlaws crouched in the back of the wagon

and returned fire, riddling the smoker and adjacent cars with lead slugs.

Gretchen saw the window shatter and Margaret's body jerked, thrown back against her.

Gretchen wrapped her arms around Margaret and lowered her, letting her lie flat on the double seat they were sitting in.

A crimson stain spread under her left breast, and Margaret groaned, her eyes squinted against the pain.

"Oh, my God!" Gretchen yelled. "You've been shot!"

Margaret moaned again and reached up to lay her palm against Gretchen's face. "Gretchen . . . Gretch . . ." She tried to speak through the blood that welled up from her lips.

"Yes, dear?" Gretchen said between her sobs.

"Tell . . . tell Leo I'm sorry . . ." Margaret rasped. Her eyes widened and she stiffened, coughing once before she died.

"Oh, no!" Gretchen screamed, burying her face in her friend's neck as she tried to squeeze life back into her.

# Chapter 15

Leo and Margaret were sitting by the banks of the Guadalupe River on the outskirts of San Antonio. The air was crisp and fresh, with an early morning ground fog covering the slow-moving current in the river. Fins of catfish could be seen as the hungry fish fed in the shallows in the shade of live oaks on the banks. The two lovers sat on a quilt with a basket of fried chicken and potato salad nearby. Leo held up a glass of red wine and toasted his new wife, his eyes shining with love and adoration.

As he put the glass to his lips and started to drink, a terrible pounding began in his head. He looked around, searching for the origin of the sound. . . .

Leo awoke, blinking sleep from his eyes. Mercifully, the pounding stopped and he buried his face in his pillow, trying to go back to sleep and recapture the joy of the dream.

The sound came again, more persistent this time, and Leo realized someone was banging on his hotel room door. With a muttered oath, he crawled from the bed, threw on a robe, and stumbled sleepily into the sitting room of his suite.

As he opened the door, he noticed Jacques come out of his adjoining bedroom, rubbing his eyes and scowling over the interruption of their sleep.

Leo pulled the door open, hearing Bill Tilghman say to Heck Thomas as they stood in the hallway, "They don't pay us enough for this, Heck."

Leo smiled, glad to see his two new friends in spite of the early hour.

"Don't pay you enough for what, Bill? To wake a body up at the crack of dawn?" he asked, waving the two lawmen inside.

Tilghman and Thomas hesitated, then they entered, their hats held before them, their faces long and serious.

Some premonition of disaster struck Leo, for his heart began to beat wildly in his chest when he saw the look on the marshals' faces.

"What is it? What's wrong?" he asked, stepping back as though to distance himself from whatever bad news the two were bearing.

Tilghman cleared his throat. "The judge got a

wire this morning, Leo. It was from Gretchen Albright."

At the sound of Gretchen's name, Jacques came forward. "Did you say Gretchen Albright?" he asked.

Heck Thomas nodded. "It seems there was a train robbery in Adair last night."

Leo took a deep breath and squeezed his eyes shut, sure now of what was coming.

Tilghman continued. "There was some shootin', an' I'm sorry to tell you this, Leo, but Miss Margaret was killed."

Leo's knees felt weak and he almost fell, but he straightened up, trying to keep tears from his eyes. "How'd it happen?"

"Bill Doolin and the Dalton Gang robbed the Union Pacific train when it pulled into the station. When the guards opened fire, the gang shot up the train. A stray bullet hit Margaret in the chest," Tilghman said gently.

"Was it quick?" Leo asked, his voice seeming to come from someone else.

Tilghman nodded. "Miss Albright said in her wire she didn't suffer none at all."

"And Gretchen?" Jacques asked hurriedly. "Is she all right?"

"Yes," Thomas said. "She wasn't hit. It was her told the judge to make sure you were notified in person. She didn't want you to read about it in the newspapers or hear any other way."

Leo, his heart turned to stone, walked over to his clothes and began putting them on. When he strapped on his shoulder holster, pulled out his Baby LeMat and checked the loads, Tilghman asked, "What are you doin', Leo?"

"You said it was Bill Doolin and the Dalton Gang that did this, so I'm going after them."

Tilghman shook his head. "You can't do that, Leo. You need to leave that job to us marshals."

Leo turned eyes filled with hate on Tilghman, making the lawman take a step back. "I'm sure Judge Parker won't let that keep me from hunting down the bastards that killed my lady."

Thomas shrugged and looked at Tilghman. "We could sure use the help, Bill, what with the other marshals all off on other business."

"Do not forget me and my shotgun," Jacques said in a voice hoarse with emotion, moving to a corner of the room to pick up his sawed-off 10-gauge.

Tilghman glanced at Jacques, still dressed in his nightshirt.

"Maybe you'd better get some clothes on first, Jacques," Tilghman drawled, "we don't want to scare the horses."

Three days later, Leo and Jacques, wearing their new deputy U. S. marshals' badges, rode with Bill Tilghman and U.S. Army Scout Charley Bearclaw through an area near the town of

Guthrie. They'd heard rumors the Doolin Gang was receiving some help from a rancher in the area, Bill Dunn.

As they neared the Rock Fort Ranch owned by Dunn, the weather turned nasty, with an early snowstorm blowing in.

The sky turned pitch black and the temperature dropped twenty degrees in a matter of minutes. Leo looked to the side of the trail and saw a plume of smoke from a structure off to the right, partially hidden in the woods.

"Hey, Bill," he called, "looks like something over there."

Tilghman reined his horse to a stop and Charley Bearclaw stopped the wagon he was riding in with Jacques.

"That's the old dugout," Tilghman said. "A kinda root cellar and smokehouse for the ranch dug out of the dirt and lined with rocks."

"Maybe we'd better go take a look," Leo offered.

"All right," Bill said. He climbed down off his horse, leaving his Winchester rifle in the back of the wagon.

"Charley, you and Jacques stay here on the trail and keep a sharp lookout. The gang could come through here anytime."

"Wonder why we have to stay out here in the

cold freezin' our asses off whilst they get to go inside where it's warm," Charley grumbled.

Jacques shrugged. "It is because you are not the big dog, my friend. It is the same all over."

"Hell, us little dogs get cold too, podna," Charley said, wrapping his arms around himself and shivering.

Bill led Leo through the underbrush toward the dugout. "Don't see no horses nor nothin'," he said over his shoulder.

He crept to the door and pushed it open before he and Leo walked inside.

At one end of the room, a large stone fireplace was filled with blackjack logs, a fire filling the room with welcome heat.

Leo glanced around at the tiers of bunks that lined both sides of the room, seeing they were hung with curtains.

There was a man hunched over in a chair in front of the fireplace, with a Winchester laid across his knees. The man looked up, a surly, uncivil expression on his face.

"Howdy," Tilghman said.

The man didn't answer. He just sat there staring at the two lawmen, his hands moving restlessly on the stock of his rifle.

"I just happened to be passing along this way with my fighting dog and thought maybe I could get Bill Dunn to match a fight," Tilghman said, making up a story to account for their bursting into the dugout. "He told me a while back he thought his dog could whip mine," he added when the man showed no inclination to engage in the conversation.

As he talked, Tilghman walked slowly toward the fireplace, rubbing his hands in front of him as if to get them warm.

The wind whistled through the rafters, rattling the wooden walls of the building, and Leo looked around again. He saw almost every bunk had a gun barrel poking out through the curtains on both sides of them.

"Hey, partner," Leo called softly, acting as if he hadn't seen anything. "We'd better get a move on before this storm gets too bad."

Tilghman glanced over his shoulder at Leo, a puzzled look on his face. Leo winked at him and inclined his head toward the door behind them. "Come on, pard, it's getting late," Leo said again.

Tilghman asked the man in front of the fire, "Guess we'd better get goin'. Which way does a fellow get out of here?"

"The same damned way he got in," the man replied, leaning to the side to spit tobacco juice into a can in the corner.

Leo and Tilghman walked out of the building and into the driving snow. "What was that all about?" he asked Leo as he pulled his coat tight around him.

"There were at least twenty guns behind those curtains, Bill," Leo said. "I'm surprised they let us out of there alive."

"They must not have known who we were," Bill said as they arrived back at the wagon.

"Drive ahead, but not too fast," he told Charley Bearclaw. "The dugout is full of outlaws."

Jacques grabbed his shotgun. "Then let us go in there and clean them out," he said, his eyes feverish with bloodlust.

"Not now," Leo said to his friend. "There's too many of them and they're too well dug in for a frontal assault. We need to get more men and come back."

In the dugout, the members of the Doolin Gang climbed out of their bunks. Bill Doolin, Red Buck Waightman, Dynamite Dick, Charley Pierce, Tulsa Jack and Little Bill were all there.

Red Buck turned angrily to Bill Doolin. "Why didn't you let me shoot that son of a bitch," he asked. As Tilghman and Leo had exited the dugout, Red Buck had aimed at their backs, but Bill Doolin had pushed his rifle barrel down.

" 'Cause Bill Tilghman is too good a man to be shot in the back," Doolin replied.

"Hell with that!" Red Buck said and started toward the door.

He stopped when he heard the hammer eared back on Doolin's six-killer and felt the barrel against the back of his head.

"I believe I'm still the leader of this gang, Red Buck, 'less you want to try and take it over."

Sweat broke out on Red Buck's forehead. He realized he was as close to death as he'd ever been in his life. "No . . . no, Bill, you're still the boss of this outfit."

Doolin eased the hammer back down on his pistol and put it in his holster. "Good. I'm glad we agree on that."

"You're wrong to let Tilghman ride outta here, Bill," Red Buck persisted. "He's gonna come back here at dawn with a big posse and we'll be trapped like rats. Now what are you gonna do about it?"

"There's nothin' for it," Bill replied. "We gotta ride outta here tonight."

"In this storm?" Dynamite Dick asked. "We'll freeze our asses off."

"Better to have 'em frozen off than shot off by Tilghman an' his posse," Doolin replied. "Now, gear up and let's shag our mounts outta here."

"Still I think I shoulda shot Tilghman," Red Buck said.

"You may just get your chance," Doolin said,

"but if you do, it'll be face to face, not from behind."

"Don't know what difference it makes, front or back, man's still gonna be dead," Dynamite Dick observed.

Doolin turned to stare at him, his eyes hard. "It makes a difference to me, Dick, an' that's all you gotta know."

# Chapter 16

By the time Tilghman had ridden back to Guthrie and gathered additional men for his posse and returned to the dugout at Bill Dunn's ranch, the outlaws were nowhere to be found.

"Let's head on back to Fort Smith an' see if there's been any news of the gang," Tilghman said, "we gotta reprovision ourselves anyhow."

When they arrived at Fort Smith, Leo and Jacques broke off from the posse and went directly to the rooming house where Margaret and Gretchen had stayed.

Gretchen, dressed in black, answered the door, her face red and tear-stained.

Jacques didn't speak. He merely held out his arms, and Gretchen immediately went into them, burying her face against his neck.

After a moment, she turned her eyes to Leo. "Her last words were of you, Leo," she said in a soft voice. "She said to tell you she was sorry."

"Sorry?" he asked, his eyes damp.

"Sorry she wouldn't be able to spend the rest of her life with you, as she'd hoped to be able to," Gretchen explained, moving away from Jacques, wiping her eyes with a handkerchief.

Leo tried to smile, though his heart was breaking. "I, too, had plans for us," he said, "plans that will never be."

"Come into the sitting room," Gretchen said, stepping to the side.

They entered the room and sat on a large, overstuffed sofa. The other women in the room, sensing their need for privacy, left quietly.

"When is the funeral?" Leo asked.

"This afternoon. Her . . . her body is coming in on the noon train."

"Do you need any help with the arrangements at the funeral parlor?" Jacques asked.

She shook her head. "No, thank you. It's already taken care of."

Leo stood up. "I'm going to take a walk. I'm sure you and Jacques have things to discuss."

As Gretchen stared at him, he added, "And, Gretchen, I'm very happy that you escaped without injury."

After Leo left, Gretchen moved to sit next to Jacques on the sofa. "It's so sad to see him like this," she said. "I can tell Margaret meant as much to him as he did to her."

Jacques took her hands in his. "Gretchen, *ma 'tite fille*, my little girl, this terrible tragedy has taught me one thing, that one should never put off saying what is in his heart, for tomorrow it might be too late."

When Gretchen started to speak, he held up his hand. "Let me finish, *cherie*, and say what I have to say in the language of my ancestors. *Je t'aime*. I love you."

Gretchen's eyes filled once again with tears and she leaned forward and kissed Jacques gently on the lips. "I love you, too, Jacques," she whispered.

"Good," he said, a look of relief on his face. "I have a very important question to ask you, *ma belle*, one that I have been aching to ask for days now."

She pulled back, a confused, hesitant look on her face. "Before you do, Jacques, there is something I must tell you."

Jacques sighed, as if he knew what she was going to say and didn't want to hear her speak the words.

"Margaret was involved with very important work at the time of her death, work that must be carried on. As her best friend, I feel it is my duty to do what I can to keep both her memory and her life's work alive."

She got up from the divan and began to pace the room, wringing her hands, tears streaming down her face, though her voice was strong and committed.

"I am going to take up where Margaret left off. I intend to travel the West, doing my best to end both the sale of liquor to young men and the use of the death penalty in the courts."

Jacques's expression became resigned and his heart grew heavy with regret. "Then I suppose that won't leave you much time for a husband, or a family?"

She came over to stand before him, her eyes looking deep into his, pleading for understanding. "No, my darling, I'm afraid it won't."

Jacques got slowly to his feet, took her shoulders in his hands, and kissed her once again, for the last time. "Then the gang of robbers have not only killed Margaret, they have murdered my dream as well."

He let go of her and gave a short bow. "If you ever tire of your crusade, there is a man in San Antonio who loves you very much and will always be waiting to hear from you."

"Thank you, Jacques, both for your love, and for your understanding," she said, placing her hand on his arm and squeezing it gently.

He nodded once, then turned and left the room without looking back, his heart feeling as if it were going to break in two.

\*　　\*　　\*

Jacques found Leo at their hotel room, packing his saddlebags for the next trip on the trail of the murderers.

Leo took one look at Jacques's face and knew he also had received bad news.

"I assume from your expression you and Gretchen will not be marrying?" he asked gently.

"No," Jacques answered shortly. "Is there news of the bandits?"

Leo fought back the questions on his lips. He knew his friend would tell him the details when he was ready. "Yes. Marshal Thomas has received word that Little Bill Raidler has been seen near the town of Tallaha and we're going there to see if we can capture him and get some word of where the rest of the gang may be hiding out."

Jacques looked surprised. "Then you don't plan to attend Margaret's funeral?"

Leo halted his packing and took a deep breath. "No, my friend, I would rather remember her as I last saw her, full of life and excitement, not lying dead in a coffin."

"I understand," Jacques said.

"I have arranged for a large floral bouquet to be presented in our names, and I sent a note to Gretchen explaining my reasons for not attending."

Jacques walked into his room and came out with his own saddlebags.

"What are you doing?" Leo asked.

Jacques's face was grim. "I am going with you. Those bandits have more than just the death of Margaret to answer for, and I intend to see that they pay the full price for what they have done to both our lives."

Heck Thomas hired two Osage scouts to help his posse find Little Bill Raidler. Howling Wolf and Spotted Dog Eater both knew the area well and were acquainted with Little Bill, able to recognize him on sight if it came to that.

Howling Wolf and Spotted Dog Eater led Thomas, Leo, and Jacques through dense woods in the hill country north of the town, while Bill Tilghman stayed in Tallaha near the telegraph waiting for further word of the gang's whereabouts.

The two Indian scouts crested a small hill and got down off their horses, followed by Thomas and Leo and Jacques, all bending low as they crowded up behind them.

Howling Wolf pointed through heavy undergrowth toward a nearby hillock. "There, see the horse tied up in those trees?" he asked.

Thomas pulled out a small telescope and peered through it. He could see the opening of a cave nestled among the trees and bushes on the side of the hill. "Yeah. He must be in that cave yonder."

Spotted Dog Eater agreed. "Yes, it is favorite place for outlaws to hide from sheriff."

Thomas pulled his Winchester from its saddle boot and jacked a shell into the chamber.

"What're you going to do, Heck?" Leo asked.

"I'm going over there and tell him to come out, an' if he doesn't, I'm gonna kill him," the marshal said.

Leo put a hand on the marshal's arm. "Would you give me a chance to try and talk to him first?"

"Why?"

"Because if he sees you, he's liable to try and fight it out, and he's no good to us dead, Heck. We need him to tell us where the rest of the gang is."

Thomas pulled a square of chewing tobacco from his shirt pocket and bit off a chunk, chewing thoughtfully for a few moments while he considered what Leo said.

He leaned to the side and spit a brown stream onto the grass. "All right, but if he makes a break for it, I'm gonna drop him."

Leo didn't wait for him to change his mind. He whirled and walked rapidly down the hill toward the cave entrance. As he went, he adjusted the Baby LeMat in his shoulder holster so it was within easy reach, and he took the badge off his coat and put it in his pocket.

He stopped fifty yards from the entrance to the cave, standing next to a thick oak tree.

"Bill Raidler!" he called, cupping his hands around his mouth. "We know you're in there. Come on out and you won't be hurt!"

Leo ducked when he saw the barrel of a rifle sticking out of the darkness of the cave. A shot rang out, the slug whining past Leo's head to slam into the tree trunk and shower him with slivers of bark.

The Baby LeMat appeared in his hand just as Little Bill jumped from the cave entrance and took aim for another shot.

Leo eared back the hammer, flicking a lever on it with his thumb that would cause it to fire the shotgun barrel. He fired from the hip, not having time to take careful aim. The pistol's center shotgun barrel exploded, sending lead pellets flying into Bill's right hand.

Sparks jumped off the gun as it was torn from Little Bill's fist and he screamed, doubling over with his ruined hand held against his stomach.

"Put your hands up," Leo called again, sighting on the man with his pistol.

Little Bill didn't answer. He ducked and ran in a crouch into the woods a few feet away.

"Go get him, men!" Thomas shouted at Howling Wolf and Spotted Dog Eater.

The two Indian scouts bounded onto their mounts and came thundering down the hill, whooping a war cry as if they were attacking Custer at the Little Bighorn.

Thomas and Jacques walked down the hill to stand next to Leo, watching the Indians course back and forth through the woods, searching for Little Bill.

"Why didn't you kill him?" Thomas asked.

Leo wagged his head. "I told you, Heck, it's Doolin I'm after and we need Raidler to tell us where he is."

As they talked, they walked over to pick up Little Bill's discarded rifle. Heck bent over, then straightened up, pushing his hat back on his head. "Well, I'll be damned. Look at that," he said, pointing to the blood-stained ground next to the Winchester.

On the ground lay three badly mangled fingers, torn off at the knuckles by Leo's shotgun blast.

Leo squatted and picked up the fingers. They were still warm.

"Damn," Thomas said, "that's gotta hurt."

"One thing is sure, Marshal," Jacques said. "It will hurt much more tomorrow than it does today."

The marshal grinned up at Jacques. "Thing like that's got to ruin your whole afternoon."

\*   \*   \*

When the Indians could find no trace of Little Bill, the posse returned to Tallaha to pick up Tilghman and continue the search the next day.

Before they took off the next morning, Tilghman asked deputy marshals W.C. Smith and Cyrus Longbone of the Bartlesville District to aid in the search.

They got a tip from a cowboy who'd seen Raidler hiding on the Sam Moore Ranch up near Pawhuska, so they headed that way.

As they rode, Leo was worried. He knew that with this many lawmen along, the chances of taking Raidler alive were slim. Longbone and Smith were two hardened men, and he knew they'd fire first and ask questions later if the occasion arose. He tried desperately to figure some way to get to Raidler before they had a chance to take him down.

The posse pulled up in front of Moore's ranch house and the cowman walked out of the door, calling a greeting to Longbone and Smith, who were known to him.

Longbone leaned crossed arms on his saddle horn. "Hey, Sam. We heard Little Bill Raidler's in the area an' we've come to arrest him."

Moore nodded, looking around at his property. "Yeah, he ain't here right now, but he usually comes strollin' down the path by the cattle corral 'bout sundown."

The lawmen looked at each other, and Tilghman pointed out places where they could hide while they waited for the outlaw to appear.

Leo walked up to Tilghman and Thomas. "Marshals, if he comes, will you let me try to talk him into surrendering?"

Thomas looked doubtful. "Leo, you already had one chance an' he got away."

"Marshal Thomas," Jacques said, cradling his shotgun in his arms. "You have five men surrounding the area. Let Leo have a word with him. I'll guarantee he won't get away this time," he said, patting the side of his shotgun as he spoke.

"It'll be our best chance to find out about the rest of the bandits," Leo added.

Tilghman glanced at Thomas and shrugged. "I don't see no harm in it, Heck. Like Jacques says, we got him pretty well covered."

Thomas looked at Leo. "You know there's a good chance he'll kill you, Leo."

Leo smiled. "It's been tried before, Heck."

"All right, but if he makes one false move, we'll drop him," Thomas said.

Less than thirty minutes later, just as the sun was going down over the western horizon, a figure came strolling down the lane. He had a bloody bandage around his left hand and a pistol tied down low on his right hip.

Leo stepped out from behind the cattle pen, ten feet in front of the outlaw.

"Little Bill," Leo said, "put your hands up, you're surrounded."

Leo had his Baby LeMat in his right hand hanging at his side.

Bill Tilghman and Jacques were in an unchinked log henhouse behind the man, while Thomas and Longbone and Smith were on the other side of the cattle pen.

Raidler's eyes narrowed and he crouched and drew his pistol, firing at the same time Leo did. His bullet passed inches over Leo's head while Leo's slug took Raidler in the right wrist, snapping the bone and blowing his pistol away.

Little Bill spun around and began running back up the trail.

Jacques and Tilghman leapt from the henhouse and let loose with their shotguns, blowing Raidler off his feet to land sprawled facedown in the dirt.

Leo ran to his side and turned him over. He was still alive but bleeding badly from six buckshot wounds, one in each side, one through his neck, two in the back of his head, and another in his shoulder. His wrist was hanging at a sharp angle, both bones apparently broken by Leo's bullet.

Moore's Indian wife ran from the ranch house with a bucket of water and a handful of clean rags. Leo took them and fashioned pressure bandages for the wounds, hoping to keep the outlaw alive long enough to tell them where his friends were hiding.

Leo had Moore bring out a wagon and fill the back with hay and quilts. The men picked Raidler's unconscious body up and laid it in the back. As they headed for town, Leo sat next to Little Bill, bathing his face with water, checking the bleeding of his wounds.

The wagon jolted over a bump in the road and Raidler's eyes opened. He gazed at Leo a moment. "Am I gonna die?" he croaked feebly.

"Most likely not, Raidler," Leo snapped. "I'm a doctor, and I'll do what I can to save your miserable life if you'll tell me where Bill Doolin and his gang are hiding. Otherwise, I'll let your blood leak through this wagon bed all the way to Tallaha. Doolin and his bunch killed my lady when they robbed the train at Adair and I aim to make him pay for it." Leo clenched his teeth. "So start talking, asshole, or you'll be painting this road red."

Raidler's eyes widened as he stared into Leo's face. From the terrible expression he saw there, he knew the man would let him die without a second thought.

# Chapter 17

The posse and the wagon carrying Little Bill Raidler arrived back at Tallaha just as dawn was breaking in the east, and Leo turned the wounded outlaw over to the town doctor for further treatment.

"You think he's gonna make it?" Tilghman asked.

Leo shrugged. "The neck wound was the worst, but I managed to get the bleeding stopped, so, barring severe infection, he should do all right."

"You manage to get any useful information outta him 'bout the whereabouts of the rest of the gang?" asked Heck Thomas around a mouthful of chewing tobacco.

"Yes. He said he'd heard the Doolin Gang planned to rob the Chicago, Rock Island, and Pacific train up near someplace named Dover."

"That ain't too far from here," Tilghman said.

"If we get on the trail right away, maybe we'll get there 'fore they hit it."

Thomas whirled around and headed for his horse. "Let's mount up, boys, an' put the spurs to those broncs. We're burning daylight!"

"Load 'em up six and six, gents, we may be in for a fight," Tilghman added as he swung into the saddle.

As the Chicago, Rock Island, and Pacific south-bound number 1 passenger and express pulled into Dover at 11:45 P.M., two men silently boarded the tender. When the train left the station, Bitter Creek Newcomb and Charley Pierce pulled Winchesters from under their long duster coats and covered engineer Gallagher and the fireman.

"Pull the train to a stop a coupla hundred yards past the water tank," Newcomb told the engineer.

Gallagher, sweating profusely and fearing for his life, applied the brakes too late and too hard, causing Pierce to stumble against the wall of the tender. When the outlaw's elbow banged against the iron, it caused him to accidentally discharge his weapon.

The bullet whined past Gallagher's head, shattering the window of the cab as it passed. Gallagher moaned and sank to his knees, sure he was about to meet his maker.

Conductor James Mack stuck his head in the

rear door of the cab. "What the hell's goin' on up here?" he asked angrily. His eyes widened as the barrel of a rifle was stuck under his chin.

"Empty your pockets," the gunman said.

Mack handed over eleven dollars and some change.

"Now get over there next to the fireman and keep your mouth shut," Newcomb yelled over the sound of the idling engine. "And you," he added, swinging the gun to point at Gallagher again, "back this damn thing back to where I told you to stop it in the first place!"

When the train finally stopped at the water tower, three more men climbed aboard—Tulsa Jack, Red Buck Waightman, and Dynamite Dick. Anxious passengers stuck their heads out of the windows to see what was going on.

One of the riflemen fired several shots at the cars and yelled, "Get your damned heads back inside them windows or I'll blow 'em off!"

The bandits marched the crewmen back to the express car. One banged the butt of his rifle against the door and demanded that the messenger inside open up.

Messenger J.W. Jones stepped back from the door. "I don't think so!" he yelled through the closed door.

Red Buck and Dynamite Dick opened fire on the door, filling it with holes from the .44-caliber slugs. Jones was hit in the left wrist and leg and fell to the floor, still clutching his own Winchester in his good right hand.

"Come on in, boys," he called, wincing against the pain of his wounds, "an' I'll fill you full of holes!"

After a moment, Bitter Creek Newcomb called, "You don't open this door in five seconds, an' we'll kill the rest of the crew."

When Jones didn't answer, the conductor was prodded with a rifle until he shouted, "Come on, Jones, you gotta open the door or they'll kill us."

Jones got painfully to his feet, leaned his rifle against the wall, and opened the door, raising his hands high. "Damned cowards," he muttered as the robbers jumped up to enter the messenger car.

The robbers pilfered the mail sacks and way safe and found no money. Bitter Creek glanced at a larger safe in the corner. He pointed his pistol at Jones. "Open her up, partner," he said, "I hear there's fifty thousand dollars in there to pay the U.S. troops in Texas."

Jones shook his head. "I can't. That safe was locked in Kansas City and it can only be opened by the express agent in Fort Worth."

Red Buck stuck his rifle barrel under Jones's chin. "You open it or I'll blow you to bits!"

Jones shrugged, his eyes narrow and hard. "Go

on and blow away, friend, but it won't change nothing. I still can't open it."

Bitter Creek turned to Dynamite Dick. "You bring any dynamite with you?" he asked.

Dynamite Dick shook his head. "Nope. It's all back at camp."

"Well, hell. Guess we're gonna have to get it from the passengers then," Charley Pierce said. "Bitter Creek and me'll patrol the rest of the train. Dick, you keep the crew covered while Red Buck and Tulsa Jack invite the passengers to contribute to our retirement."

The men nodded and all took off to do their assigned tasks.

Red Buck stuck his gun in a porter's back and had him proceed down the corridor ahead of them, carrying a large sack.

Former U.S. Deputy Marshal William C. Grimes was in the second passenger car. When he heard the bandits making their way through the cars, he took out his gold watch and stuck it under his seat.

Tulsa Jack came abreast of Grimes and grinned. "Ah, howdy there, partner," he said, recognizing the marshal and thumbing back the hammer on his Colt. "We meet again. Guess I've got you this time. Out with your dough."

Grimes fished in his pocket and handed over $1.40.

Tulsa Jack scowled and waved his pistol around. "You'd best be better supplied next time I rob you." He turned to the man across the aisle. "Hand it over," he growled, stuffing Grimes's money in his pocket.

"You are playing on a dead card here," Lew Fossett said.

Red Buck grunted and stuck his gun in another man's face. "Give me all you got," he said roughly.

"But I just got outta the penitentiary an' don't have hardly enough to eat on myself," the young man cried, handing over two dollars.

Red Buck grunted and handed him back a half dollar. "Here, this'll buy you breakfast," he said.

As they walked up the aisle, one older lady put a five-dollar bill in the sack. Tulsa Jack tipped his hat and retrieved her money, handing it back to her. "We are not here to rob or molest women. We came to rob the express company, but have failed and need a little expense money. We will confine ourselves to males in levying this tax."

All in all, the bandits only took about four hundred dollars and a few watches in the robbery. As they walked back down the aisle, Tulsa Jack paused before Grimes. "Give my compliments to Chris Madsen," he joked.

When they got to the cab, Red Buck stuck his pistol in the engineer's gut. "Wait till you hear a gunshot from the southeast," he said, " 'fore you start her up."

The gang of five climbed down off the train and mounted the horses they'd reined next to the tracks, riding off into the night with a series of whoops and yells.

Tilghman, Thomas, Leo, and Jacques were having troubles of their own. Another freak early winter storm had blown in, gusting winds in their faces and sleet mixed with snow making further progress impossible. They decided to camp in a grove of blackjack oak trees which would give them some shelter from the freezing temperatures.

After they made camp and built a huge fire, Jacques bundled in blankets, wrapping his ground sheet around him. "First the sun boils my brains and the next day a norther freezes my balls off. I hate this damned country!" he said, rolling over with his back to the fire and his head on his saddle.

Tilghman held his tin coffee cup with both hands, trying to get some warmth in them as he and Leo and Heck Thomas sat as close to the fire as they could get.

He glanced at Jacques, then at Leo. "You and your partner make a strange combination," he mused.

Leo smiled. "Yes, I guess we do. I was raised in the lap of luxury by rich relatives in New Orleans. We lived on the north side of town in a section called Society Row. My mother and uncle were constantly forbidding me to go near the wharves and docks of the seamier side of town, sure I'd get my neck cut or suffer some other indignity."

Leo paused to refill his coffee cup as Tilghman lit a cigar with hands shaking from the cold. "Of course, being a normal boy, I did exactly what my elders told me not to, and began to sneak out of my room after they were asleep in order to prowl the rougher parts of town. One night, as I walked along the docks admiring the clipper ships in the harbor, a gang of toughs surrounded me and began taunting me and calling me a society sissy. As I prepared to fight all six of them, knowing I had no chance against so many, this short, ragamuffin sort of boy about my own age stepped from the shadows. He took one look at the terrified expression on my face and came to my side. 'Leave him alone, he ain't done nothin' to you,' he said to my tormentors. They paid him no mind, evidently thinking his small size meant a lack of fighting ability. Before I knew it, Jacques and I were embroiled in a fight for our lives. After we'd managed to knock several of the boys down, the leader of the gang pulled a stiletto from his belt, saying he was going to cut our gizzards out."

Tilghman paused, his cup halfway to his mouth. "So they meant business, huh?"

"Yes. The wharves of New Orleans bred some pretty tough men and boys in those days. Anyway, just as I was about to soil my pants, Jacques LeDieux laughed, pointing at the boy's blade. 'You call that a knife?' he asked and he pulled a twelve-inch Bowie knife from his boot."

"A Bowie knife?" Thomas asked, smiling.

"Yeah, and it was almost as long as his arm in those days," Leo replied.

"What happened?" Tilghman asked.

Leo shrugged. "The boys ran away into the night, and Jacques and I have been friends ever since. We began to meet at midnight and prowl the docks together, seeing what mischief we could get into, as young boys are wont to do."

"And you been together ever since?" Thomas asked, glancing again at Jacques.

Leo nodded. "Marshal, it's not every day you find friends like Jacques, men you can depend on to stand by you no matter the consequences."

"You got that right," Tilghman agreed. "Why, I can count on one hand the men I call friend."

"Me, too," Thomas said, " 'cept I'd still have a couple of fingers left when I was done."

\* \* \*

By the time the storm let up and Bill Tilghman, Heck Thomas, Jacques, and Leo were able to make their way to join the hunt for the Doolin Gang, Marshal Chris Madsen had arrived on the scene and was organizing a posse to go after the robbers.

"The gang didn't bother to cover their tracks," Madsen told Thomas and Tilghman. "I heard they hoped we'd follow 'em so's they could bush-whack us."

Tilghman looked at Thomas and grinned. "Then let's give 'em a chance to do just that," he re-marked, climbing back into the saddle.

They took off after the robbers at daybreak, finding it easy to follow the gang's trail in the mixed snow and ice on the ground from the storm of the previous day.

At two o'clock in the afternoon, Leo and Jacques, riding in the lead, crested a hill on the edge of a sand basin.

"Look, Leo," Jacques said, pointing, "there's their horses."

There was one man guarding the mounts, with the rest of the gang asleep in a small grove of blackjack oaks.

As Thomas and Tilghman and the others came over the hill, the guard looked up and saw them. They could hear him shouting to the others as he jumped in the saddle.

"Throw up your hands, you sons of bitches," yelled Marshal Thomas, snapping off a quick round with his Winchester.

The robbers leaped to their feet and began firing wildly at the posse as they struggled to get on horseback.

As the posse charged down the hill, the bandits scattered among the oak trees, receiving and returning fire as fast as they could pull their triggers.

Men rode wildly among the grove of trees, back and forth through the din of gunfire and the clouds of acrid gunsmoke that soon covered the area like a dense fog.

Leo and Jacques rode close together, giving each other cover as bullets whined and screamed, shucking bark off trees and pocking the ground around their horses' hooves.

Suddenly, out of the smoke a man came riding right at them, firing his pistol as he leaned over his saddle horn.

Leo reached out and knocked Jacques off his horse and out of the line of fire as the man thundered past, his bullets imbedding themselves in the saddle on Jacques's horse.

Leo tried to get his rearing, crow-hopping horse under control as the man galloped away, firing back over his shoulder.

Finally, Leo twisted in the saddle and snapped

off a shot with his Baby LeMat, firing more by instinct than by aim.

His slug took the man in the back, entering his right side, going through his heart, and coming out under his left arm.

Red Buck, seeing his friend shot off his horse, jerked his reins and turned his mount toward Leo, riding at him hard and fast, a pistol aimed at Leo.

Jacques whipped his beloved Ange to his shoulder and fired both barrels, blowing Red Buck's horse from under him.

Red Buck tumbled to the ground, rolled, and came up on his feet.

Bitter Creek Newcomb, seeing Red Buck afoot, swung his horse around and rode to him, leaning down with his arm extended.

Red Buck grabbed the arm and swung up behind Bitter Creek, who never slowed as he hightailed it for deeper cover in the blackjack forest.

The fight lasted forty-five minutes, and over two hundred shots were fired. After the remaining robbers fled, Thomas called a halt, figuring the posse's horses were too tired to continue the pursuit.

He walked over to the dead man lying on the ground and stood over him, his hands on his hips until Leo and Jacques rode up.

"Looks like you done robbed your last train, Tulsa Jack," he muttered to the corpse.

He glanced at Leo. "That was a helluva shot you made back there, Leo," he observed.

"Even a blind pig'll find a root once in a while, Marshal," Leo said, watching blood run from Tulsa Jack's body to pool in the dirt and snow next to him.

"After seein' you shoot that six-killer in your hand, won't nobody ever call you blind," Thomas added.

Jacques showed Leo the holes in the saddle from the outlaw's bullets. "That was a close one, *mon ami*," he said.

"Looks like you fell off that horse at just the right time," Leo said, smiling.

"Looks like," Jacques said, returning the grin.

# Chapter 18

Judge Parker answered a knock on his door at precisely ten o'clock on Saturday morning. He was sure it would be Dr. LeMat making their appointment, and it pleased him that LeMat would not be late.

"Ah . . . Dr. LeMat. Please come in."

LeMat carried an easel, a canvas, a painter's palate and a small black case containing his paints.

LeMat grinned. "I'm looking forward to this," he said, "as I hope you are."

Parker closed the door. "I've never sat for a portrait, so I don't know what to expect. Please choose the place you want by any of the windows."

"A sitting is merely what the name says. All you have to do is sit," LeMat told him, selecting a window where the most sunlight would shine on his subject. "Pick a chair to your liking and place it where the sun strikes your face."

Mary came into the room when she heard their

voices. She nodded once to Dr. LeMat. "So good to see you again, Doctor. I hope you brought the list of foods my husband can eat. He's been feeling dizzy more often the past few days."

"Good morning, Mrs. Parker. Indeed I did make a list of foods and ways they can be prepared. I'm afraid it's a short list. However, control of eating habits is the only way to treat diabetes. Medical science lags far behind in studies of this disorder and the condition, as I told you before, can be quite serious."

"I do not want to lose a leg or go blind," Parker said with a dry note in his voice. "Surely there is something on your list I can enjoy."

LeMat grinned again. "Perhaps not, Judge," he said, setting up his easel. "As a rule of thumb I told my patients that if it tastes good, spit it out."

"You have a black sense of humor, Doctor," Parker said, carrying a chair to a square of light cast on a rug below an eastern window. "Shall I prepare to dine in the stable with our horses on oats and hay?"

"You'd be a far healthier man. No more dizzy spells," LeMat replied, obviously enjoying Parker's discomfort.

"I think I'd rather be dizzy," he said, sitting down with his face turned toward LeMat, "although the loss of a leg or my eyes may force me to change my mind."

LeMat handed Mary a piece of paper.

"My goodness," Mary said, reading down the page. "Oatmeal with no brown sugar. Pancakes with no syrup. No sugar in your coffee or tea. No more cakes, pies, or puddings. You've had the last of your favorite peanut butter cookies as well. Lemonade without sugar. You may have all you want of cooked vegetables and meat. Bread, but no jelly."

"How dreadful," Parker said. "I think I'd rather be dead. No peanut butter cookies? I'm quite certain now that I'd rather be dead."

"You have a choice to make, Judge," LeMat said, staring him in the eye, serious now. "A choice between a longer and healthier life, or the alternatives I described."

Parker glanced out the window at the gallows platform. "I may ask George Maledon if he'll hang me instead. I'll pronounce sentence on myself and order my own hanging. My last wish will be a plate full of my wife's cookies and sweetened lemonade."

"Hush that sort of talk, my dear," Mary said. "I'll find things you like that you can eat." She scanned the list again. "What on earth is red-eye gravy?"

LeMat placed his canvas on the easel and sat down. "An alternative to cream gravy on biscuits," he said, taking out a piece of charcoal to begin outlines of Parker's face. "You can use bacon or ham, however the judge cannot eat any of it since fat becomes sugar in the bloodstream. Use a modest portion of the drippings, add flour and a cup of coffee while stirring it over heat. The result is delicious over biscuits and it won't cause your blood sugar to rise." He looked past the canvas to Parker. "Your expression is one of deep melancholy, Judge. I know the list of foods may be bad news. Your face is as long as a coon dog's front leg. Please try for a more serene countenance."

Parker took a deep breath. "I've just been told I can't enjoy what I eat any longer. No more cookies or pies, and yet you want me to accept this with serenity, as you put it, and smile nicely at my fate."

"I'm only trying to keep you alive, Judge," LeMat said. "Turn your chair a little bit to the left. I'm beginning with your eyes, as I told you I would. Try to think of something pleasant while I work."

"Like peanut butter cookies," Parker muttered.

His brush strokes were deft, short, employing the art taught to him by George Catlin, Parker supposed. He sat there thinking about the gun battle LeMat had joined with his deputies, the skill he demonstrated with a pistol, according to Heck

Thomas. It was more than a passing oddity, how a physician could have so many other talents . . . a knack for shooting, steady nerves under fire, a sense of purpose many of his questionable deputies lacked when bullets began to fly. And now this, another side of the man, a gentle painter who concerned himself with proper angles and the right light, the look in a subject's eyes.

*Strange*, Parker thought.

Another curious side of LeMat was his choice of traveling companions, the hawk-faced Cajun who seemed as out of place on the Western frontier as any man could. Heck had said the Cajun was a magnificent fighter, an excellent marksman who showed no signs of fear.

*They seem to have nothing in common*, Parker thought, as LeMat studied his face for a moment before he returned to his canvas.

Now Parker gazed at a bookshelf in front of him, wondering if he would survive the doctor's diet. He had a passion for good food, and a craving for sweets that was soon to be denied him. A pancake without syrup or honey was like eating warm sawdust, and would sit just as heavily in the stomach.

They sat around the coffee table while Mary poured them tea. Parker tasted his. "How awful. Tea without sugar is too terrible to describe."

"It will be better in the summer, when you may add lemon juice," Leo said.

Mary ignored her husband as she handed Leo his cup. "How will I know if the diet is working, Dr. LeMat?" she asked. "I've made a shopping list for the market including the things you said my husband can have."

Leo hesitated. "The only test of this diet's success may strain the bonds of your matrimony," he replied.

"And how is that?" Mary asked.

"Your husband's urine."

"Dear me. I don't understand."

"You must taste it. If it's sweet, he's getting too much fat or sugar."

Mary gave her husband a sideways glance, then she looked back at Dr. LeMat. "Taste it?"

"Place the tip of your finger in a small sample."

"Enough!" Parker exclaimed, waving the notion away with his hand. "We'll find another way. If I'm feeling better we can assume the diet is working. I won't have my wife tasting the contents of a chamber pot."

"As you wish, Judge," LeMat said, draining his teacup. "It is, sadly, the only way to be sure."

"We must move on to another topic," Parker said. "Tell me about the train robbery. Marshal Thomas has already given me some of the details."

"We were under heavy fire, but the gods smiled

down on us. We were lucky. A stray bullet could have taken any one of us down."

"I understand your . . . associate, Mr. LeDieux, is quite good with his shotgun."

"Jacques is experienced in that sort of thing. He came from one of the roughest parts of New Orleans. He's not lacking in nerve."

Mary sat down, looking at the likeness of her husband's dark eyes on the canvas. "If you'll pardon me for saying so, Dr. LeMat, Mr. LeDieux has the appearance of a ruffian."

"In many respects he is, Mrs. Parker. He cannot shed his violent beginnings. But he is intelligent, with a boundless curiosity. I taught him more formal English. When I met him, he spoke a combination of French and Cajun slang. Over the years Jacques has become an excellent cook, with French cuisine as one of his specialties. He never prepares an unfit meal."

"Let's stop talking about food," Parker said, releasing an audible sigh. "I am doomed to a lifetime of sentencing men to death and foraging for my survival like a cow among stacks of hay and grain."

Leo chuckled. "It won't be that bad, Judge," he said, as he came to the end of what he hoped to accomplish for the day, standing while he wiped his brush with a cloth. "You'll soon develop a taste for other foods. And you'll feel so much better the restricted diet will be worth it."

"Highly unlikely on both counts," Parker said, as Leo carried his easel and canvas to a corner of the room.

Leo put his brushes and oils away. "I intend to go after this Bill Doolin," he said, ambling back over to Parker and his wife. "I rarely ever let personal sentiment take a hand in affairs involving the use of my gun, but in this case an exception will be made."

Parker nodded. "You'll have the full authority of a federal marshal's badge, Dr. LeMat. Doolin and the criminals who ride with him are a top priority."

Leo stiffened. "You may not be as pleased with the result, Judge," Leo said coldly, a subtle change in his voice.

"And why is that?" Parker asked, puzzled by the doctor's remark.

Leo stared out a window briefly. "Because I intend to kill him," he answered softly. "If I have my way, he's one murderer you'll never have the chance to hang."

"This is because of Miss Margaret's death, I presume?"

Leo refused to reply. He walked over to a coat rack and took down his hat. "Thank you for the tea," he said to Mary, "and to you, Judge, for being so patient with the sitting. I may be out of touch this week. Jacques and I will try to pick up Doolin's trail."

"I wish you luck," Parker said. "While I am not an advocate of violence in the common sense, there are a number of criminals in my jurisdiction who understand nothing else."

"I'll see you next Saturday," Leo said, making a move toward the door.

Parker decided it was time to lighten the mood. "Perhaps you can come over for dinner at the end of the week to discuss your search for Doolin. I'll be interested to know how close you can get to him. We'll be having a bale of the finest hay to be found in Fort Smith, and whatever else my poor wife can find on your list that won't strike me blind."

Leo evidenced no appreciation of his attempt at humor when he said, "I intend to have Doolin's body at the undertaker's before the week is out."

Mary's face paled as Parker stood up to offer Leo his hand. "Godspeed, Dr. LeMat."

Leo shook with him and let himself out, climbing down the stairs. Parker closed the door behind him.

"Did you see his face when he talked about Bill Doolin?" Mary asked softly.

"I did," Parker replied. "Dr. LeMat has two personalities, it would seem. I enjoy the man who came here to paint my portrait and discuss my health. However, after meeting his other side, I wouldn't want to be on the other side of Le-Mat's gun."

"He must have loved Margaret very much," Mary said, stepping to the window to watch Leo walk away.

Parker joined her, his hands on her shoulders. "I can only imagine how he must feel. If I lost you, my dear, I'm afraid I would also be on the trail searching for revenge, just as the doctor is."

"I hope he finds peace instead," Mary said, slowly shaking her head.

# Chapter 19

Judge Parker addressed the men in his office. Marshals Heck Thomas, Bill Tilghman, Leo, and Jacques were standing before him as he read from a wire on his desk.

"I received this wire from Chris Madsen this morning, gentlemen," he said, peering at them over his half-rim glasses. "He says he's heard rumors that either Bill Doolin or some of his gang have been spotted up near Beaver Creek. The Chicago, Rock Island, and Pacific has a train coming through with an army payroll on board. They sent guards, but it may not be enough if Doolin is up to his old tricks. He's said to have as many as ten men riding with him."

"Did Madsen say if he was plannin' on headin' up that way?" Bill Tilghman asked.

"No," the judge replied. "He just had a double murder in a barroom fight and he's busy securing an indictment so he can transport the men here."

Parker leaned back in his chair, his eyes on Leo. "I want you men to go up there and check out his report." He hesitated a moment. "I'm well aware that all of you have reasons for wanting to see Doolin arrested, but you need to remember you're acting under the authority of the United States government, and I expect you to act accordingly." This last remark was addressed to Leo, a fact made clear by the way the judge's eyes bored into Leo's.

Tilghman put his hat on. "Come on, men. We got some serious ridin' to do. Beaver Creek's a two-day ride from here, an' that's if the good weather holds."

As the four men rode past the outskirts of Fort Smith, the sun came out from behind gray clouds and burned away the ground fog. The day dawned bright and clear and cool only days after one of the worst snow storms of the year.

Jacques glanced at the sky. "I will never understand the weather out here. It seems to go from hot as hell to cold as the bottom of a well without so much as a 'by your leave.' "

Leo grinned. "You continually complain about the weather, Jacques, but you never *do* anything about it."

"Were it up to me, *mon ami*, everyplace would have the same climate as New Orleans. I never saw snow until you dragged me out here to this godforsaken wilderness."

"This year ain't been so bad," Heck Thomas opined as he rode next to Jacques. "Why, I remember times in the old days when it got so cold, men sitting around a fire would have to thaw out their words so's they could hear what each other was saying."

When Jacques gave Thomas a doubtful look, Tilghman added, "That was the same year I stopped by the trail to take a piss and it froze into one long icicle 'fore it hit the ground. Hell, I had to build a fire 'fore I could break it off and get back on my horse."

"This is a joke," Jacques said, uncertainty in his voice.

Leo laughed as Tilghman continued. "Hell no, Jacques, it's the straight truth. Matter of fact, I was trailin' a man at the time an' the snow was so deep I just followed the furrow his horse left an' the edges were damn near over my head."

The banter continued in this fashion for most of the day, with the tales getting taller as the day wore on.

Just before dusk, clouds rolled in from the north and there was a suggestion of ice on the wind, and the marshals decided to make camp while there was still light, before the temperature began to drop.

*    *    *

After supper, the four men sat around the campfire, smoking and drinking brandy from a bottle Jacques had bought at a saloon before leaving town. A light snow had begun to fall, causing Jacques to make more remarks about how miserable a country this was.

Leo looked over at Tilghman. "Bill, I'm somewhat of a student of the West, and I've read a lot about you and Heck Thomas since you became marshals, but I've not heard much about your early days out here. What was it really like?"

Tilghman glanced at Thomas and smiled. "It was a lot different back then. About the only law west of the Mississippi was what a man carried on his hip, or in his rifle boot."

"How did you manage to get into the peace-keeping business, Bill?" Jacques asked, using the brandy bottle to adjust the mixture in his coffee, then handing it to Tilghman.

Tilghman added a dollop of brandy to his coffee cup and took a sip, as if thinking about how to put things.

"When I was about eight or so, my father went off to fight in the Civil War, and my older brother, Richard, became a drummer boy. I was left alone as the 'man' of the place. Let me tell you, it was quite a job for a boy of eight to help keep food on the table, plow the fields with an old mule, bring in the crops, and take care of my mother at the same time."

Leo took a cigar out of his coat pocket and put a match to it, leaning his head back and blowing smoke at the clouds overhead, trying to see if the snow was slowing any. "I can see it must have made you mature quite early."

"Yep, an' it didn't help any when my dad came back from the war blind and my brother married and moved away."

"What did you do?" Jacques asked.

"The only thing I could do. I kept workin' the farm and takin' care of mom and dad. Then about two years later, this was in the summer of '72, I got work as a professional buffalo hunter. I'd become a pretty fair hand with a rifle, shotgun, knife, an' pistol during my years takin' care of the farm, so the work kinda came natural to me."

"I've read stories about the old buffalo hunters, Buffalo Bill Cody and Wild Bill Hickok, and I've met Wild Bill Hickok, but I never had a chance to ask him about the old times," Leo said. "What was the life like?"

"That summer me an' a group of men made a camp near where the Kiowa and Bluff creeks come together, 'bout fifty miles from Dodge City. We built a dugout large enough for all fourteen of us, and one for the horses an' mules, too. After a while, we'd just about shot all the buffalo for miles around, so we moved southward and made another similar camp on the Kiowa Creek. Now, just south of there was the Cimarron River on the edge of the Gloss Mountains, home of the Cheyenne."

Tilghman stopped to pull a cigar out of his pocket and put a lucifer to it, while Thomas reached over and relieved him of the brandy bottle.

"Now, the Cheyenne just naturally resented us white men comin' in an' shootin' up all their buffalo. One day, when we got back from an afternoon of shootin' damn near everything in sight, we found the camp destroyed . . . tents shredded, equipment smashed, and everything just generally torn up."

Jacques glanced at Tilghman. *"Mon Dieu!* Did you leave?" he asked.

"The other men wanted to, but I was a young buck, full of piss an' vinegar, an' probably a bit big for my britches as boys are sometimes.

"Anyway, like I said, to me the attack was a personal insult, an' I wasn't about to stand for it. So, after the others took off, I hid in some tall pampa grass near camp, figurin' the Injuns would come back to see what we'd done."

He took a drag on his cigar, a sip of his brandy and coffee, and continued. "Sure enough, I'd only been there a couple'a hours when three of 'em came back. One of 'em had a rifle, but the other two only had these long, nasty-lookin' knives. When they saw me, they charged right at me, whoopin' and hollerin' to beat the band. Guess they figured it'd scare me off like the others."

"And did it?" Jacques asked, forgetting all about his coffee, letting it get cold, untouched on the ground before him.

"No, sir. I let the hammer down on my shotgun, and a full double-load of buckshot hit the lead one in the stomach, killin' him right away. The second one, seein' my gun was empty, ran up at me with that big knife in his hand, figurin' on gettin' my scalp. I clipped him hard under the chin with the butt of the shotgun and knocked him on his ass, unconscious. The third one jumped on my back, intent on cuttin' my throat an' we wrestled around a bit 'fore I was able to turn that knife into his own neck."

"What happened to the one you knocked down?" Leo asked.

Tilghman chuckled. "When he got up an' saw what'd happened to his friends, he took off runnin' an' never looked back."

"I'd venture a guess that you had no further problems with the Cheyennes on that hunt," Leo said.

"Nope," Tilghman replied. "As a matter of fact, a few days later we had the best hunt of the year at that particular spot."

"So the other hunters returned after you'd gotten rid of the Indians," Jacques said.

"Yeah. They showed up the next day, all carryin' their big Sharps buffalo rifles, ready to do some damage."

"What caliber Sharps did you use?" Leo asked, interested, since he'd read several stories about the gun called the Sharps Big Fifty, a .52-caliber weapon.

"I didn't use a Sharps," Tilghman replied. "I used a shotgun."

"A shotgun?" Leo asked, astounded. "How in the world could you hope to kill a buffalo with a shotgun?"

Tilghman laughed. "You sound just like my old huntin' partners. They asked the same question. I made some special loads for my shells. Instead of buckshot, I substituted a single lead slug in the shell."

Tilghman glanced at Leo. "You'd know why if you'd ever fired a Sharps. I didn't much like the way the Sharps kicked. I was afraid it'd knock me off my feet or give me a broken shoulder."

"That's for damned sure," Thomas interrupted. "Damn things kick like a mule."

"And did it work?" Jacques wanted to know, thinking back to the times in his younger days when his grandfather had to put a poultice on his shoulder after he fired a 10-gauge shotgun at some bayou ducks.

"Only too well," Tilghman replied. "The best thing was, I could fire while ridin' my pony, without having to jump down an' fire from the ground like my partners. In less than half an hour that first day, I'd bagged a dozen buffalo. I guess the number I got total that year was over four thousand, while the combined total of all my partners taken together was less than half that."

"And," Leo asked, smiling, "did they then start using shotguns?"

"Oh, yeah. 'Fore long, all of 'em wanted to use shotguns 'stead of Sharps."

Jacques tasted his cold coffee, made a face, and got up to throw some more grounds in the tin pot next to the fire. When he had it heating, he returned to his place by the flames and asked, "What did you do after you gave up buffalo hunting, Marshal?"

"When the buffalo got scarce, sometime around '75, I rode on over to Dodge City, just to see what was goin' on. I met Charlie Basset, who was sheriff of Ford County, an' he asked me if I'd consider bein' his deputy." Tilghman shrugged. "Heck, I didn't have nothin' else goin' on, an' I'd never been a lawman before, so I said I'd give it a shot."

"Wasn't Dodge City rough back then?" Jacques

asked. "I've heard it was difficult to sleep at night because of all the gunfights going on."

"You might say that. On my second day on the job I had a run-in with a local gunman named Texas Bill. When he saw my shiny new badge, he stepped in front of me on the boardwalk and blocked my path. I told him, 'You'll have to turn your guns in or leave town. It's a new ordinance.' "

"Did he draw on you?" Jacques wondered, enjoying the tales of towns he'd only heard about from Leo's reading.

"Not then. He just said, 'Never heard of it. If you want 'em, come an' take 'em from me.' "

"Did you?"

Tilghman smiled. "Being new to the job, I didn't quite know what to do. It seemed a small thing to shoot a man over, so I just punched his lights out, an' then two of his buddies jumped on me an' I had to punch them out, too. Once they was all out cold, I got some folks to help me carry 'em to jail."

"Those were tough times in Dodge," Leo said.

"You're right, Leo, an' it went from bad to worse. In early '76, Mayor Dog Kelly, who owned the Alhambra Saloon, wired Wyatt Earp over at Wichita to come to Dodge an' take over from the town marshal. Old Dog had heard a bunch of Texas cowboys were on their way to Dodge an' he didn't think Bat Masterson an' I could handle it alone."

"So that's how Wyatt got to Dodge?"

Tilghman nodded. "He brought Neal Brown an' Bat's brother, Ed, with him."

"I assume things quieted after that."

"Yes, but it weren't easy. Back then the town was full of toughs, men like Doc Holliday, Ben Thompson, and even the worst of 'em all, Wes Hardin. After a while, Bat Masterson was elected sheriff of Ford County an' hired me to stay on as his deputy."

"What was it like working for Masterson?"

"It was all right, but I soon tired of it an' home-steaded me a few hundred acres, built me a cabin, an' married a widow-woman named Flora Rob-inson. I partnered up with Neal Brown an' just took life easy for a while."

Leo wanted to ask more about the wild days Tilghman had lived in, but noticed Heck Thomas trying to stifle a yawn across the fire.

He took a final drink of his brandy and stood up. "Well, Marshal, this has been interesting, but I see your partner is about to fall asleep. We'd better call it a night."

Tilghman glanced at Thomas, a chagrined look on his face. "Sorry, Heck, hope we haven't bored you to death with all this talk about the past."

"Oh, no," Thomas protested. "It brought back

some good memories of my own, but Leo's right. We're gonna have to hit the trail awful early to make Beaver Creek in time to do some huntin' tomorrow." He stood up, covering his mouth over another yawn. "Maybe we'll be able to continue the stories on the ride tomorrow."

"I'm done wore out talkin' 'bout myself, Heck, but maybe you can tell Leo and Jacques about the time we spent up in Hell's Half Acre in Perry," Tilghman said.

"Was Perry as rough as Dodge City?" Jacques asked, reluctant for the stories to end.

"Well," Thomas said, smiling at Tilghman, "it was a boom town with a hundred and ten saloons and twenty-five thousand citizens who didn't particularly like having to contend with laws and such."

"Jacques, can't you see the marshals are dead tired?" Leo asked. "Let's let them get some sleep and maybe they'll finish the story tomorrow."

Jacques held up the brandy bottle and turned it upside down, showing it was empty. "It's just as well. We've finished the brandy so I might as well go to sleep."

# Chapter 20

As the engine of the Chicago, Rock Island, and Pacific Railroad train rounded a bend, Bill Doolin spurred his horse and bolted from his hiding place in a thick copse of woods near the track.

He leaned over the saddle horn, chilly evening air almost taking his hat off, and fired his pistol at the engineer at the controls, hoping to distract him from the men hiding up ahead to stop the train.

His horse was gamely giving it everything it had to keep up with the engine, racing along at almost twenty miles an hour, when its right front leg hit a gopher hole and it swallowed its head and did a somersault on the hardscrabble dirt next to the tracks.

Doolin went flying ass-over-elbows through the air, dropping his pistol and grabbing his head to protect it, sure he was going to die. He hit the ground in a rolling, twisting tumble, landing thankfully in a thick bush of sage and weeds, which cushioned his fall.

He got to his feet, limping a little on his right foot as he searched the nearby ground for his pistol. Once he found it, he ran hobbling over to where his horse stood, its right leg cocked with no weight on it.

He soothed the frightened animal for a moment, and then he swung up into the saddle, praying the animal's leg wasn't broken. He put the spurs to it and it took off at a slower pace, but at least it could still run.

As he moved toward the train in the distance, he heard a loud explosion and saw a sheet of flame leap skyward, lighting up the darkness of approaching dusk.

"Yonder he is!" a voice cried.

Bill Doolin swung his horse toward the yell, feeling it flounder underneath him . . . he would need another horse to make it away from the train after they got the money, for his bay was too badly crippled from its fall galloping beside the tracks, and it stood no chance of making it to the Kansas border. After the dynamite explosion derailing the Chicago, Rock Island, and Pacific train to Beaver Creek, all was confusion, made worse by the darkness and the snow.

A pistol cracked on the far side of the tracks

near the railroad bridge. Seconds later, the shot was answered by the roar of a shotgun, echoing off rocky cliffs where the train lay in pieces, twisted wreckage everywhere, flames licking up the sides of the overturned locomotive, giving off an eerie yellow light.

"You bastard!" Doolin hissed, clamping his jaw, figuring the shotgun had been fired by a marshal at one of his men in the brush beyond the rails. For the moment he forgot about the army payroll in the baggage-car safe. He decided it was worth a bit of extra time to make damn sure the marshal was killed. If he could, he meant to do it himself.

He rode past the pellet-riddled body of Carl Hardin and gave it no thought, other than a slight touch of regret that one of his men wouldn't make it to Kansas. These were the risks of the train-robbing profession, something his men should have understood by now.

"I see him!" a high-pitched voice shouted. "He's next to that bridge support over . . ."

A thundering explosion ended Jimmy Ballard's warning before he got it all said, when the marshal took aim with his scattergun and fired.

Now, more determined than ever to see to the lawman's demise, Doolin spurred his laboring mount directly toward the bridge. He saw a horseman dash past the wrecked passenger car with a pistol aimed in front of him.

"Soldiers!" someone bellowed from the ravine where the baggage car came to rest. Doolin glanced over his left shoulder.

Five men in dark uniforms came spilling from the baggage car with rifles in their hands. Doolin's hopes were quickly dashed that the derailment would kill or seriously injure most of the army guards watching the payroll. He'd been warned that these were seasoned veterans riding this train, not the green recruits so often encountered in the past when they hit other trains from St. Louis and points east.

A rifle barked somewhere near the locomotive and one of the soldiers went down in a heap. A second shot was just as successful, sending a uniformed man sprawling on the ravine bottom as his rifle fell from his hands, his scream of pain and terror echoing shrilly across the hills.

Then a pistol went off, four shots fired as quickly as a revolver could shoot, and one more soldier slumped out of sight in the darkness, either hit or deciding that discretion was the better part of valor.

Doolin returned his attention to the bridge where he'd last seen the federal marshal. His horse was barely able to hold a gallop as he came within less than a hundred yards of the bridge supports.

In an instant when the light and shadow was

just right, he saw a shape move near one of the timbers. He cocked his Colt and fired too early, his slug taking a piece of wood off the piling but not drawing any blood. He decided to wait until his horse brought him closer to the movement he glimpsed, the outline of a man, where he could get a clearer shot.

His horse almost fell when it crossed loose stones and yet he continued to spur it relentlessly, caring nothing for the animal, his only thought to end the lawman's life at any cost.

A blossom of bright light flared underneath the bridge and his bay tumbled to the ground as the sound of the blast came seconds later. Shotgun pellets ripped tiny holes in Doolin's left shirtsleeve and tore off his hat, a few stinging his cheeks as he was thrown over the downed horse's neck for the second time that night.

He landed with a grunt in some thorny brush, yelling as the thorns dug into his flesh and ripped his clothes. Cursing, he ignored the pain from his fall and the minor shotgun wounds to scramble to his feet with his pistol clamped in his fist. He was stunned momentarily, unable to locate the right bridge support where he'd seen the muzzle-flash. His vision was double at first and he reached up under his hat to feel an egg-sized knot on the back of his head.

He shook his head and blinked, trying to clear his vision before going again after the marshal.

From the east a six-gun spat flame, popping, sending a stabbing finger of orange-yellow light toward the bridge. And then a scream of anguish followed, when a man staggered away from one of the timbers with both hands pressed to his stomach, a shotgun lying on the ground behind him where he'd dropped it when he was hit.

"I got him!" Bitter Creek Newcomb cried.

Doolin let out a sigh and lowered his pistol even as another gun battle raged near the baggage car. He watched the wounded marshal sway and stumble a few steps more, until a man on a horse rode up to him and fired at his head.

The lawman whirled and his head snapped back, jolted by a bullet's impact, and then he went down on his knees as if he meant to pray.

"Attaboy, Newcomb!" Doolin shouted, a twisted grin lifting the corners of his mouth.

The marshal fell over on his chest and lay still, just as Bitter Creek jerked his horse to a full stop. "He's a dead son of a bitch, boss! You ain't never seen so much blood!"

Doolin's attention returned to the money. "Get over to that baggage car an' help 'em kill the rest of them soldiers. I've gotta find me a horse someplace."

Newcomb trotted his horse over to Doolin, smoke still curling from his revolver. "Carl ain't gonna be needin' his no more. In case you didn't know, the law dog gunned him down."

"I saw it," Doolin said, remembering the way Carl had been blown off his horse. "Go help the rest of the boys an' then let's open that safe."

"You want me to fetch you Carl's horse?"

"Not just yet. I'm gonna walk over yonder an' look right close at that marshal . . . just to make goddamn sure the sumbitch is dead."

"I shot him square in the face, boss."

"Get goin'. I'm gonna make sure."

Doolin trudged over to the railroad bridge and looked down at what was left of the lawman's head. Bitter Creek's shot had gone plumb through the marshal's skull, being as it was fired at such close range.

"I hope the goddamn worms eat you," Doolin spat at the still corpse as steam slowly rose from the pool of blood around the body in the chilly air. "You got just what you deserved, bounty-huntin' asshole. . . ."

Dynamite Dick blew the safe. The explosion sent the roof of the baggage car skyward in a thousand swirling pieces. As the noise died down they could hear bits of sheet metal and wood pattering to the ground all around the train wreck. In a moment of silence that followed, Doolin heard a passenger whimpering somewhere in the darkness, the voice of a woman crying. He looked toward the sound, resisting the urge to go to her and tell her he was sorry, that he didn't intend no harm to come to women, that she was just in the wrong place at the wrong time.

"Get the money loaded!" Doolin snapped, sending Lefty and Dick and Cotton Polk rushing toward the ruined baggage car with canvas bags. Cotton's brother, Raymond, held their horses, attempting to settle the terrified animals after the huge explosion. One side of the baggage car had been blown to bits, while the other somehow remained upright, its naked timbers standing up against the night sky like the skeleton of some animal on the desert.

"Sure hope that safe door got blowed off," Raymond said in his typical matter-of-fact way. Nothing ever seemed to excite Raymond Polk, not even counting money.

"You can bet on it," Doolin replied. "That was enough dynamite to blow this whole train to hell."

"Counted ten dead soldiers, boss, an' Newcomb said he killed that star-packer. Both trainmen is dead. Ain't seen no sign of the conductor, but I don't figure he'll give us no problems now that he don't have the soldiers to back him up."

Doolin wondered idly how many passengers

had been killed in the derailment. He wished there were some way to do the job without hurting innocent people, but there just wasn't. "It was one hell of a wreck, Raymond. An' we just made ourselves one helluva payday," he yelled, putting such thoughts of compassion out of his mind.

Raymond glanced over his shoulder at the night around them. "Never was one to worry too much, boss, but the Rock Island ain't likely to stand for no more of this. Next time they'll hire a whole army of bounty hunters, men who know how to shoot, an' we'll be goin' up against some bigger numbers, the way I got it figured. We hit this railroad mighty hard in the pocketbook. They won't make it this easy fer us again."

Doolin nodded, for he'd been thinking the same thing himself for months. "That's how come this is our last job for a spell, Raymond. We'll have more'n enough to last us up in Kansas for maybe a year."

"If there's really six thousand in that safe," Raymond said as though he doubted it. "That'd be our biggest haul since we took up robbin' trains."

"There'll be six thousand," Doolin told him. "My source ain't been wrong about the money yet. Six thousand was just too temptin' to pass up."

"It's damn sure a bunch of money," Raymond agreed. "Lefty said we got all them soldiers. I reckon that's how come they was on this train in the first place, on account of it was so much loot this time."

Doolin nodded again. "When I first heard it was six thousand I figured the railroad was baitin' us, like they aimed to set a trap for us someplace. But we scouted the whole damn rail line an' there wasn't nobody. The railroad had to believe that havin' so many soldiers on board was enough to handle us, or to scare us off tryin' to rob the train." He gave a dry chuckle, his lips curled in a grin. "We damn sure proved 'em wrong about that."

"Too bad about Carl," Raymond said, as he saw Cotton jump down with bags of money in each fist. "He was a good man to have sidin' with us."

"Yeah," Doolin agreed, "he'd do to ride the river with, all right."

"His luck ran out," Frank said, shaking his head. "Cain't ride the owl hoot trail without luck, that's for sure."

"Jimmy's hurt bad. Bleedin' from a hundred holes when that law dog shot him with that express gun of his. He may not make it. Newcomb stopped some of the bleedin' an' had to help him climb on his horse, but I don't know if he'll be able to stay in the saddle for long without no help."

Doolin recalled hearing Jimmy Ballard scream when the lawman shot in the direction of his voice. "He'll have to stay in the saddle by his lonesome," Doolin said. "We gotta get to the line quick as we can. Ain't got time to do no babysittin', 'cause sure as hell somebody's gonna be comin' after us for what we done tonight."

Lefty and Dick followed Cotton out of the ruined railroad car carrying more bags of money.

"Seems kinda cold, Bill, not to help Jimmy. He's been with us right from the beginnin'."

"Every man in this outfit knows the chances we're takin'," Doolin said in a hard voice, looking around at his men. "I ain't bein' cold about it, just practical. We can't slow down for just one man who's hurt. Kansas is the only place where we'll be safe and Jimmy knowed it. When a man eats lead in this business, it comes with the job sometimes."

"Sure wish it hadn't been Jimmy," Raymond said.

Doolin gave him a cold stare. "You'd rather it'd been you, Raymond? Or your little brother?"

"Never said that, boss. Just said it was a shame to leave him if he can't ride."

Dynamite Dick was the first to reach the horses. He had four sacks stuffed with currency, two in each hand. "You shoulda seen what that dynamite done!" he cried, handing bags up to Raymond and Pierce. "Some of the banknotes got burnt, but hell, you ain't never seen so much cash in all your life."

Dick gave four sacks to Sonny Jones to tie across his saddle while Cotton trotted over to Clyde Devers with three bulging bags of bills. Doolin turned to mount Carl Hardin's horse when he saw Josh Walker riding toward them leading Jimmy Ballard on his pinto, slumped over the pommel of his saddle.

Doolin got aboard the brown gelding, gathering his reins just as Josh and Jimmy rode up.

"He's bad hurt, Mr. Doolin," Josh said, aiming a thumb over his shoulder at Jimmy. "Bleedin' like a stuck hog."

"Bring him along, so long as he can stay in the saddle. If he falls off, we gotta leave him." He gave the men around him a hard stare. "You boys know it can't be no other way. One man can't be the cause of the rest of us gettin' caught. Now let's ride!"

Men turned their horses away from the train, forming a single file across a stretch of snow-covered hills behind Doolin, thus to leave as few tracks as possible for the law, or the army, to find when they came to investigate.

The train wouldn't be reported missing until sometime tomorrow, when it didn't arrive at Beaver Creek. Even then, a rider would have to be sent to old Fort Carson, an abandoned army post where a few cowmen and goat ranchers lived, in order to send a telegram to St. Louis to inform the railroad office that the train failed to show up.

"I got it figured there's more than six thousand here," Dynamite Dick said. "Damn, you never seen so much money in one place at one time."

"We'll count it tomorrow mornin' after we cross the line into Kansas," Doolin explained.

"Can't believe we're so rich."

Doolin scowled at the dark hills, heading for an old Osage Indian trail they followed to reach the Beaver Creek area. "We ain't got to Kansas yet," he warned. "Keep your eyes open an' your mouth shut, just in case we missed an army patrol when we scouted this place before sundown."

"We'd have knowed it if soldiers was here," Dick said as he rode behind Lefty.

"I sure as hell hope you're right," Doolin said.

"Hold up a minute!" Josh cried at the rear of the procession. "Jimmy can't sit this horse no longer. I been holdin' him up fer a spell, only he's out cold now."

"Push him off an' keep his horse," Doolin ordered, raising his voice more than he wanted, so Josh could hear him. "Take his guns before he falls."

"Sure seems cold," Raymond Polk muttered again, as the thud of a body sounded from the darkness behind them.

# Chapter 21

Heck Thomas came from the telegraph office, his eyes afire and his teeth bared in a fierce grin as he held a piece of yellow paper in front of him.

Tilghman, who was waiting for him with Leo and Jacques, muttered, "Huh, looks like the old dog is on the scent of our boy."

Leo had to agree. Thomas, in the past few weeks, had become more and more obsessed with arresting or killing Bill Doolin. To Leo, it seemed a dangerous state of mind to be in while hunting a man as dangerous as Doolin. Like a physician doing surgery, Leo felt one must try to maintain some objectivity when tracking a killer, lest you end up being the one killed. Rage and hatred interfered with the coolness needed when doing an important job of any kind.

Though Leo had even more reason to hate the mad-dog murderer Doolin, his mind was clear and he refused to let his personal animosity cloud his judgment. He could only hope Thomas would do the same in their upcoming chase or else Doolin would get the chance to have even more blood on his hands.

"Well, boys, it seems Doolin's been sighted up near Lawson," Thomas said, holding up the paper from the telegraph office.

"Lawson?" Leo asked. "Why would he be up there?"

Tilghman smiled, though there was precious little humor in the expression. " 'Cause, that's where his wife and in-laws live," he answered.

"I figured Doolin was too smart to let a skirt lead him into a trap," Thomas said.

"Perhaps he is thinking with his little head instead of his big one," Jacques observed dryly.

Tilghman shrugged. "Word is, the wife had his baby not too long ago, a little girl I believe. Maybe he wants to pay 'em a visit 'fore headin' out on the owl hoot trail again."

He glanced at Thomas. "How'd you find this out, anyway?"

Thomas grinned. "I spread the word around his old stompin' grounds that the reward for Doolin's capture or death would be shared with anyone giving word of his whereabouts or that helped us capture him."

Tilghman nodded at the wire. "An' someone actually took you up on that?"

"Yep. A couple of blacksmiths in Lawson, Tom and Charlie Noble, sent me this wire. Seems young Charlie is courting Bill Dunn's younger sister, an' Doolin's wife an' baby are stayin' at her parents' house near the Dunn ranch."

"Well, what are we waiting for? Let's shag our mounts and get on the trail," Tilghman said.

Aware that most of the folks in Lawson were—if not outright friends of Bill Doolin and his gang—sympathetic to their flight from lawmen, Thomas advised Tilghman, Leo, and Jacques that they'd better stay under cover as they watched and waited near the Dunn ranch for Doolin to show up. They kept a close watch on the Elsworths' home, the parents of Doolin's wife, hoping to catch a glimpse of the outlaw if he showed up to visit his family.

Leo and Jacques, who were not known as lawmen in the area, were used to go into town and buy supplies and such as the group settled in for a possible long wait. They were warned not to ask too many questions about Doolin, or someone would warn him they were on his trail.

Tom Noble, when approached by Heck Thomas, said that Doolin had been to the Elsworths' house for at least an hour or two each of the past three days.

"I also seen his wife Edith an' her father load

up a wagon with a plow, furniture, and other personals as if they was plannin' on takin' a long trip somewheres," the young Noble told Thomas.

"Why don't you get your brother to ask around at the Dunn ranch an' see if he can find out what Doolin's plans are?" Thomas asked.

Tom Noble nodded and said he'd get right on it, but he'd have to be careful not to arouse any suspicions or Doolin might kill him.

A cold rain was pouring down as Charlie Noble sat with Rosa Dunn in the kitchen of her parents' ranch house. They were eating apple pie and drinking fresh milk.

The back door to the house opened and Bill Doolin stepped inside. He stood there a moment, shaking water off his fish, the yellow slicker all cowboys kept in their saddle bags as protection against just such weather.

"Howdy, Bill," Charlie said around a mouthful of pastry, holding his glass of milk up in a greeting.

"Hello, Charlie, Rosa," the outlaw replied as he hung his slicker and hat on the wooden rack next to the door and wiped his boots off on the mat.

"What are you doing here?" Rosa asked, hero worship shining in her eyes.

Charlie tried to keep a scowl off his face. He wasn't all that happy about the way his sixteen-year-old girlfriend thought Bill Doolin was so special. To him, the man was nothing more than a cold-blooded killer who didn't deserve the respect all the townspeople of Lawson seemed to give him. Hell, it didn't take no special skills to shoot people down like dogs, he thought with jealousy burning in his breast.

"I just came to talk with your brother Bill," Doolin replied. "Me and Edith are fixin' to head out for New Mexico to make a fresh start." He grinned. "Time to shake these law dogs off my trail."

Charlie lowered his face and stuffed more pie in his mouth to keep Doolin from seeing the dislike cloud his expression and give his feelings away.

After Doolin passed through the kitchen toward the sitting room where Bill Dunn and his wife were reading, Charlie stood up, wiping his mouth with a linen napkin.

"I gotta go, Rosa," he said, getting his own hat off the rack.

"But you haven't finished your pie, Charlie," Rosa said, "and it's raining cats and dogs out there. Why don't you wait for the storm to pass before you leave?"

Charlie shook his head, thinking about what his brother Tom had said about the marshal needing to know what Bill Doolin was planning.

"Can't," he said shortly, pulling the brim of his

hat down tight against the wind gusting outside. "I'll see you tomorrow," he muttered as he ducked out the door and ran through the driving rain toward his horse tethered outside, his boots splashing in the gathering puddles.

Marshal Heck Thomas answered the knock on the door of the old line shack he and his posse were using as shelter while they kept watch on the town.

Tom Noble stood there, his hat in his hand. "I got word on Doolin," he said, stepping through the door, looking around with a worried look on his face.

Leo, Jacques, and Tilghman sat up, taking notice of his words.

"Yeah? What'd you find out?" Thomas asked.

"That offer for a share of the reward money still good?" Noble asked.

Thomas nodded. "It is if you help us catch the son of a bitch," he replied.

"He's planning on picking his wife and baby up later on tonight. They're headin' up to New Mexico in that wagon she packed the other day. Says they're gonna make a new start so as to get the law dogs off his trail."

Thomas looked over his shoulder at Tilghman. "Well, us law dogs'll have to see about that."

He glanced back at Noble. "Where're they gonna meet?"

"At the Elsworth house, where his momma- and papa-in-law live."

"Thanks, Tom. We'll be ready," Thomas said, a fierce grin on his face.

Unlike the previous night, the evening sky was clear and cloudless, with a bright moon shedding light over the prairie near the Elsworth house. Leo and Jacques were on the north side of the house, hunkered down behind some bales of hay placed near the stable as feed for the Elsworth horses, while Tilghman and Thomas were on the other side of the house, near an old pigpen where they could get a clear look at the trail going past the house.

Suddenly, from out of the gloom, Leo saw a figure walking down the path, leading his horse by the reins, a Winchester rifle held in front of him with both hands.

"He must be suspicious," Leo whispered to Jacques, "see the way he's looking back and forth, checking all the shadows as if he knows we're here."

Jacques nodded, silently. "It is too late for him, my friend, for he is already in the jaws of our trap," Jacques whispered in reply, earing the hammers of his shotgun back as he spoke.

Leo cocked his Baby LeMat, fingering the lever

on the hammer which would cause his shotgun barrel to fire when he pulled the trigger. The moonlight and darkness would make shooting the .44 barrel too risky a shot at this range.

A yell came from near the pigpen. It was Heck Thomas, calling, "Stop! Throw up your hands!"

Doolin whirled around, letting go of the reins and raising his rifle toward the voice.

Leo stepped from the shadows into moonlight. "Give it up, Doolin," Leo called, holing out his Baby LeMat as Jacques followed him into the open, his shotgun already up against his shoulder, the sights on Doolin.

Doolin swung the Winchester toward Leo and snapped off a shot, the bullet passing between Le-Mat and Jacques, embedding itself in the bale of hay behind them.

Doolin's rifle must have jammed, for he dropped it and jerked a pistol out of his hip holster and fired off another three rounds as fast as he could pull the trigger, crouching so as to make a smaller target.

Leo had no choice. He pulled his trigger and the Baby LeMat exploded, shooting flame and buckshot from the barrel to light up the night.

Jacques and Tilghman and Thomas all fired seconds later, sending a volley of slugs toward the outlaw.

Doolin spun, hit by a dozen rounds, took two

steps, then he was blown off his feet to land spread-eagle on his face in the dirt.

From the porch behind them, Leo could hear Edith Doolin scream, "Oh, my God, they've killed him!"

While Jacques turned and pointed his shotgun at the house to make sure no one interfered, Leo walked to the body, keeping his LeMat aimed at the fallen man in case he wasn't dead yet.

He turned the dead man over and examined him. He was riddled with gunshot wounds, and out of morbid curiosity, Leo counted them. He found twenty buckshot wounds, four of which were over the heart. His left arm had a bullet wound which appeared to have come from Tilghman's Winchester, for Thomas, Jacques, and Leo had all fired shotguns.

Even in death, the gunman's eyes were dark and penetrating over thin lips and canine teeth. Leo shivered, glad to be quit of the man who'd murdered his dream.

Jacques walked softly up behind Leo and stood over the body.

"*C'est assez, fils de la putain!* That's enough, you son of a whore," he spat at the dead man, his eyes dark with thoughts of what might have been had this man been killed sooner.

Leo stood up. Strangely, he felt no joy at the man's death, just a numb feeling in his heart. He tried to remember the author of the old saying, "There is a world of despair in the words 'if only.' "

Jacques stepped over to his friend and put his arm around Leo's shoulder. "It is finally over, *mon ami*," he said gently. "Let us go back to Fort Smith."

Leo leaned his head back and stared at the moon shining brightly in the evening sky, blotting out the stars with its light.

He shook his head. "No, Jacques," he replied in a soft voice. "It will never be over as long as Margaret lives within my heart. She will remain alive as long as there are friends who remember her beauty and passion."

Jacques nodded, his thoughts going to his own loss and how neither of them would ever be the same after this trip.

# Chapter 22

Heck Thomas, Bill Tilghman, Leo, and Jacques were shown into Judge Isaac Parker's chambers as soon as they arrived at the federal district court on their return from the killing of Bill Doolin.

"Come in, gentlemen. Have a seat," Parker said, his face more relaxed than Leo had ever seen it. *His color is better, too,* Leo thought, observing the man with his trained physician's eye, *and he appears to have put on some weight recently*. Perhaps the diet was doing him some good after all.

Parker took a bottle of brandy from his desk drawer and poured them all shots into water glasses. He looked over his spectacles at them and, to the surprise of all of them, actually grinned, an expression seldom seen on Parker's face, especially in his chambers.

"Just a short nip to cut the trail dust," he said, though Leo noticed he didn't pour himself any of the liquor, probably due to his strong religious convictions rather than out of a concern for his diabetic diet.

Parker leaned back in his high-backed leather chair and laced his fingers together over his stomach. "I received your wire stating the posse had achieved its purpose, Heck," the judge said as Leo and Jacques sipped the brandy while Heck and Bill Tilghman drank theirs down in one swallow.

Heck glanced at Leo and Jacques before replying. "Yes, Your Honor, though unfortunately, the suspect was killed when we attempted to apprehend him."

The judge's face sobered. "I assume he gave you no choice in the matter?"

"No, sir," Tilghman replied. "We ordered him to surrender twice, and he answered us by firing on us several times, barely missing Leo and Jacques with his first rounds. We gave him every opportunity to give up, but he chose to go out with his guns blazing."

"And, you're sure this man you shot is Bill Doolin?" the judge asked.

"Yes, Judge," Leo answered. He pulled a daguerreotype from his coat pocket and handed it across the desk to Parker. "We had this picture made of the corpse, and, in addition, Doolin's wife Edith identified the body."

Parker peered through his glasses at the body, lying on its back with multiple gunshot wounds to his face, neck, and chest. His clothes were spotted with dark stains where his blood had seeped out. "It seems from the number of wounds, you men took no chances with this desperado."

Thomas grinned for a moment, then forced his expression to become more sober. "No, sir. We had him surrounded, and when he fired at us, we all let loose at the same time."

"It would appear none of you missed," Parker observed drily, glancing from one to the other.

The clerk stuck his head in the door. "It's time to begin the afternoon session, Your Honor," he said.

Parker stood up and pulled on his robe. "Once again, you gentlemen have performed your duty admirably, under difficult circumstances." He pulled several sheets of vellum paper from another desk drawer and handed them to the four men seated in front of his desk. "These are certificates of appreciation for the fine work you've done."

Leo glanced at the certificate. It was done on heavyweight paper and featured fine engraving under the seal of the Federal District Court of Oklahoma Territory. It had all their names on it and a short message saying they had performed valuable service for their country at great risk to life and limb. Leo carefully folded it and put it in his coat pocket. It was a memento he would always cherish.

"Leo, I will see you this evening at my house," Parker said as he made his way toward the door. "I believe we have some unfinished business to attend to?"

"We do," Leo answered. "I'll just take an hour or so to finish up my portrait."

The judge peered at him over his glasses, his hand on the doorknob. "I would invite you to dinner, but I fear you would be better served to eat elsewhere, since the cuisine at my house is less than appetizing lately."

Leo smiled as Parker ushered them out of his chambers through a side door.

The four men paused on the street outside the court, and Heck and Bill stuck out their hands. "It was a pleasure working with you, Leo and Jacques," Bill Tilghman said.

"Yeah," Thomas agreed as they shook hands all around. "I'd never have believed a picture painter could shoot like that, Doc."

"Wait until you see his portrait of the judge," Jacques said with a grin. "Then you will say you can't believe a shootist can paint like that!"

The marshals touched their hats and walked off toward the nearest saloon.

Leo looked at Jacques. "I'm going to get something to eat. How about you?"

Jacques's face flushed a bright red. "If it is all

the same to you, *mon ami*, I would like to say my good-byes to Mademoiselle Gretchen."

"Of course, Jacques. I'll meet you back at the hotel later."

Jacques sat on the sofa next to Gretchen, holding both her hands in his. "Are you sure you will not change your mind, *cherie*?"

Gretchen shook her head, her eyes shining from unshed tears. "No, my love. I have already made arrangements to meet with Carrie Nation in Washington for a rally next month. We are going to do our best to get the government to pass a law forbidding the sale of liquor to minors."

Jacques looked down at their intertwined hands. "If that is what will make you happy, then I hope you succeed. I know Miss Margaret would approve."

Gretchen squeezed his hand as hard as she could. "If only you knew how hard it is for me to leave you, Jacques. It is truly something I wish I could avoid."

Jacques shook his head and stared into her eyes. "No, no, *ma 'tite fille*, my little one, do not fret over me. You must do what your heart tells you to do, and no matter how much I want you with me, I want you to be happy for the rest of your life."

"Thank you, dearest, for being so understanding."

Jacques got to his feet and took her in his arms. He kissed her gently on the lips. "Good-bye, *'tite belle*, sweetheart," he said, his voice husky with desire and longing, his thoughts on what might have been.

"Good-bye, my darling," she replied.

Leo knocked on the door and Mary Parker opened it, bidding him to enter.

Leo had his preliminary sketches under his arm and laid them gently on a side table before he took off his hat.

He walked into the sitting room and found Judge Parker sitting, staring out of the window.

"Another rough day, Your Honor?" he asked.

Parker turned serious eyes to him. "Yes. Two young men, barely out of their teens, were tried for murder. I had to sentence them to death."

Leo nodded, knowing how such verdicts upset the judge. "You are a Methodist, I believe?" Leo asked.

Parker looked puzzled by Leo's question, but nodded his head.

"Then, you must be aware one of the doctrines of your religion is the concept of free will, Judge."

A small smile curled Parker's lips, as if he knew what Leo was leading up to.

"As such, we are all endowed by our creator with the choice of how we will live our lives,"

Leo said. "The two young men, no matter the circumstances, had the free will to kill or not to kill. If they chose to kill, then they must be held accountable for their actions, both here and in the Hereafter," Leo concluded, moving toward his painting, which stood on an easel in the corner near the window.

Parker gave a small chuckle. "You sound just like my wife, Doctor LeMat, trying to cheer me up at the end of a difficult day."

Leo shrugged and removed the sheet draped over the painting.

Both Judge Parker and his wife Mary walked over to look at the painting.

Mary clasped her hands to her chest. "Oh, look, dear," she said.

Leo had fully captured the depth of compassion that dwelt within Judge Isaac Parker's eyes. It was a fine likeness.

Parker nodded. "Do I look that old, my dear?" he asked Mary with a small smile.

"No," she said, shaking her head and taking his hand. "You look that distinguished."

Leo took the canvas off its frame and rolled it up, putting it in his valise. Afterward, he took his sketches and opened them, placing them on the frame for the judge and his wife to see.

"These are not quite as good, but I think they will do nicely if you have them framed," Leo said.

"Oh, yes," Mary said, smiling at the portrait of her husband. "You have captured the kindness in his eyes that only I get to see."

"The men I sentence would disagree with you, I fear," Judge Parker said.

Leo shook his head. "It is no contradiction to have a heart filled with compassion and kindness and to still be able to do one's sworn duty, Your Honor," he said.

He gathered his things and stuck out his hand. "I am honored to have met you, Isaac Parker," Leo said.

"And I you, Doctor LeMat," Parker replied, taking Leo's hand in a firm grip.

# Chapter 23

When Jacques woke up the next morning, he walked into their hotel sitting room, stretching and yawning.

He found Leo busily packing their bags. "Why the hurry, Leo?" he asked, hoping Leo wouldn't notice the redness of his eyes from his sleepless night thinking of Gretchen.

Leo pointed to a newspaper lying on the sofa in their sitting room. "Have you read this morning's papers?" he asked, excitement in his voice.

Jacques frowned. "No, Leo, I most certainly have not. Why?"

"I see where the notorious bandit, Black Bart, has been apprehended by James Hume in California," Leo said.

"I have heard of Black Bart, the scourge of Wells Fargo. But who is James Hume?" Jacques asked as he picked up the paper and began to read.

"Hume is the first of a group of men Wells

Fargo calls 'special operatives,' " Leo answered as he threw shirts and socks into a valise. "These men work as undercover detectives for the stage line, both to apprehend robbers and to ferret out embezzlers that work for the company. Another one working for the company is Fred Dodge."

"Don't tell me you are planning to paint these men's portraits?" Jacques asked.

Leo straightened up. "Why not?" he asked, as if he'd never considered not doing so. "What could be more romantic than working undercover in the wild West to bring stage robbers to justice?"

He took the paper from Jacques and turned the page. "And just look at the picture of these two. Have you ever seen more distinguished features?"

Jacques sighed heavily. "And these men reside in California?" he asked.

Leo nodded. "Of course."

"And is there a train that runs from Fort Smith westward to California?" Jacques continued.

Leo thought for a moment, then wagged his head. "I'm afraid not."

"And so, does this mean we are going to be traveling by stage rather than by train?" Jacques asked, a plaintive note in his voice.

"Of course," Leo replied, "at least until we get far enough west to catch a connecting railway."

"And I suppose it will not be possible to hook our special train car up to these stages?"

"No, don't be silly," Leo said, wondering what had gotten into Jacques this morning to make him so irascible.

"Leo, do you realize how difficult it will be to make our coffee inside a moving stage coach?" Jacques quipped, throwing up his hands in despair.

# Author's Note

Hell on the Border was the name given to the federal jail in Fort Smith, Arkansas, by inmates and was essentially as described in our novel. The Oklahoma Territory was likewise called Hell's Fringe, and it easily lived up to its grim description.

With the exception of Leo LeMat, Jacques Le-Dieux, Margaret, and Gretchen, all of the major characters in this novel actually existed and lived in and around Fort Smith, Arkansas, in the latter part of the nineteenth century.

Judge Isaac Parker, the Hanging Judge, served for twenty-one years on the Fort Smith bench. During that time, he tried 13,490 cases, of which 9,454 resulted in guilty pleas or convictions, and 160 men were sentenced to die. Seventy-nine men were hanged from the gallows on the courthouse grounds. Though few people outside his own family were aware of it, he suffered from diabetes mellitus. On September 1, 1896, with Parker confined to his sickbed, his clerk solemnly arose in his courtroom and called out, "Oyez! Oyez! The Honorable District and Circuit Courts of the United States for the Western District of Arkansas, having criminal jurisdiction of the Indian Territory, are now adjourned forever. God bless the United States and the honorable courts!"

The Wild Bunch, as the Doolin Gang was also known, consisted of Bill Doolin, George (Bitter Creek) Newcomb, Oliver (O1) Yantis, William (Bill) Dalton, Bill (Tulsa Jack) Blake, Charles (Dynamite Dick) Clifton, George (Red Buck) Waightman, Roy Daugherty (Arkansas Tom Jones), William F. Raidler (Little Bill), and Richard West (Little Dick). At the time of Bill Doolin's death, only Dynamite Dick and Little Dick West were left of the infamous Wild Bunch. They went on to join the Jennings Gang, but soon left for various reasons. Dynamite Dick was killed by deputies on November 7, 1897, near Checotah, Oklahoma. Little Dick West was killed by Heck Thomas and his posse on April 8, 1898, thus ending the saga of the Wild Bunch.

The three guardsmen:

Henry Andrew Thomas, known to all as Heck, worked as a deputy marshal in Oklahoma Territory between 1893 and 1900, where he met the other two guardsmen, Chris Madsen and Bill

Tilghman. In three years these men arrested more than three hundred wanted men. Heck Thomas was wounded over six times in gunfights while doing his duty. After his stint in Oklahoma Territory, Thomas moved to Lawton, Oklahoma Territory, in 1902 where he served as chief of police for seven years. He retired in 1909 and died in 1912 of Bright's disease, the same illness that killed Judge Parker.

William Matthew Tilghman, after leaving his marshal's job in the Oklahoma Territory, served as sheriff of Lincoln County, Oklahoma Territory, in 1900, as chief of police of Oklahoma City in 1911, and later was persuaded to come out of retirement in 1924 to clean up Cromwell, Oklahoma. It was while on this job a drunk prohibition officer, Wiley Lynn, shot and killed the seventy-year-old Tilghman as he led him to jail.

Christian Madsen, after leaving his marshal's job at Guthrie, Oklahoma Territory, joined the Rough Riders and went to Cuba to fight in the Spanish-American War. After returning from Cuba, Chris reentered law enforcement and in 1911 was appointed U.S. marshal for Oklahoma. From 1918–1922, he was a special investigator for Oklahoma governor J.B.A. Robertson. He died in a retirement home at the age of ninety-three.

George Maledon, known as the "Virtuoso of the Rope," was a towering Bavarian giant who carried out sixty executions for Judge Parker. He also had a chilling reputation as the "Prince of Hangmen," as the local press dubbed him. He dressed all in black, and was tall and lean and seemed to enjoy his role as hangman for the Hanging Judge of Fort Smith, Arkansas.

Except for minor changes for dramatic effect and the inclusion of our fictional characters, the exploits of these famous lawmen and outlaws, and the events they participated in, were portrayed as accurately as possible. In fact, their lives, and in some cases their deaths, were such that fiction could hardly improve on them.